Bat

The Piper Anderson Series
Book 6

Danielle Stewart

Copyright Page

An *Original* work of Danielle Stewart.
Battling Destiny Copyright 2014 by Danielle Stewart

ISBN-13: 978-1503269712

Cover Art by: Ginny Gallagher
Website: www.Ginsbooknotes.com

Books By Danielle Stewart

Piper Anderson Series:
Book 1: Chasing Justice
Book 2: Cutting Ties
Book 3: Changing Fate
Book 4: Finding Freedom
Book 5: Settling Scores
Book 6: Battling Destiny

Piper Anderson Extras:
Choosing Christmas - Holiday Novella - Chris & Sydney's Story

Betty's Journal - Bonus Material(suggested to be read after Book 4 to avoid spoilers)

Saving Love – A Piper Anderson Novella

The Clover Series:
Hearts of Clover - Novella & Book 2: (Half My Heart & Change My Heart)
Book 3: All My Heart
Book 4: Facing Home

Dedication

To the mothers. My mother and all of the mothers of the world. For every hour of sleep you've given up, every tear you've shed, and stretch marks you wear. However a child has come into your life whether by birth or by you opening your heart to one who needs you, know that you are a hero. You have the power to shape a mind, warm a heart, and change a life.

Be someone's Betty…

Synopsis

Michael Cooper has his life together. He is the successful lawyer all his friends turn to when they find themselves in trouble, and he and his beautiful wife just welcomed their newborn daughter to the world. In just under two years, he went from a cocky bachelor to a quintessential family man with a close-knit group of friends. Yes, Michael Cooper has his life together. Until the news that his father has died forces him to return to his hometown in Ohio.

Any feelings of grief and loss over his father are overshadowed by the idea of having to step back into a world he has spent years trying to forget. He knows, all too well, the reach of his mother's manipulation and the grip of his father's spiderweb like empire. It took everything he had to leave Ohio all those years ago and make a life for himself in Edenville, NC. Now, in the wake of his father's death, will he have the strength to leave it all behind again? Will Jules, the one woman who understands him the most, stand by him when the truth about his family comes to light? Can Michael battle the destiny that's been thrust upon him and make his way back to the simple life he's fought so hard to build?

Prologue

Growing up I never thought I'd be the kind of man who didn't grieve his father's death. But how can I *pay my respects* to a man who lost my respect years ago? Yet, no matter how little I feel for him, the same driving force that shaped most of my actions when I was younger somehow is overtaking me once more. The unwavering need to keep up appearances was drilled into me at an early age. That's what my family has always been about. No matter how deep the secret or how ugly the truth, we'd polish ourselves up, put on our public faces, and pretend we had it all.

It's why I continue to go through the motions even though I don't feel an iota of sadness at the news of my father's sudden passing. The only emotion I muster is annoyance. His death has taken me away from the life I love, from my wife and daughter. I've never missed anyone the way I miss them right now and every minute I'm gone I'm creating a rift that won't be easy to repair. I've thrown my marriage into flux just to come to my birthplace to bury my father, and it makes me hate him even more.

I sling my small travel bag over my shoulder as I exit the airport and wave off the man offering to cart my luggage. I have no luggage because I'm not staying. I will not be here long enough to unpack. I'll buy a suit, or wear one of the ten I'm sure my mother has had tailor-made for me. She'll likely have that many because she doesn't know my size, considering we haven't seen each other in nearly seven years.

It would be easy for me to have a car service drive me to my parents' house. They'd know the way.

Everyone in this city knows where my parents live. Or I could have easily called my mother and had one of her drivers retrieve me from the airport, but on principle I go to the noisy curb and hail a cab. It's a statement I'll be making to my mother. I am not like my family anymore. I don't need every flashy accessory or their lifestyle perks. I'm happy with simpler things. That's where joy lives in this world, between the lines and underneath the flashy superficial. Life happens when you connect with people, not constantly working to be better or have more.

Leaving my wife and daughter without so much as a word to come out here is eating me alive. But I don't regret it. Whether Jules ever forgives me or not, I know I made the right choice. I'm keeping them safe.

Chapter One

"I've known her half my life and she's never gone this long without talking. I didn't even think she was capable of the silent treatment," Bobby whispered with a grimace but not quietly enough.

"This isn't the silent treatment," Jules interjected as she struggled to fasten Frankie's diaper with one hand and grab a pacifier with the other hand. She'd already been feeling like things were too much for her and now she might have to start doing this alone. It was great timing, she supposed, as she imagined her life as a single mother. Maybe that was being dramatic but she couldn't help it. "I have nothing to say. There is a difference."

"You always have something to say. It's genetic." Bobby tentatively stepped across Betty's sitting room and took a seat next to Jules as she laid Frankie down on her play mat on the floor. The rhythmic humming of the mat's music had comforted Jules as many times as it had driven her nearly to the brink of insanity. Much like Michael.

"What is there to say? Michael is gone. One phone call and he's gone. It's not like I'm stupid. I can see the writing on the wall. It's my own fault really." Jules knew this would draw the disagreement of everyone in the room, but she didn't care. Since Bobby had told her Michael had left, she'd spent every second trying to understand what had happened. How it happened. But now she knew.

"Don't say that, Jules," Piper insisted, the first to try to make her feel better about the disastrous situation. "You don't really know what's going on. None of us do."

"You're making my point for me." Jules slipped her hands into the sleeves of her oversized sweatshirt and pulled her legs up as she curled into the corner of the couch. "I don't know what's going on with my own husband and that's my fault. I realized something wasn't right with Michael's relationship with his family, but I ignored that. I never asked a single question. Shouldn't I have pushed the topic, demanded to know why I hadn't met his parents and sister? Why they hadn't come to meet Frankie, for goodness sake? What do any of us really know about Michael? Next to nothing. I tried to pretend everything was fine, and I got what I deserved for that complacency. Now his father is dead, and he takes off for Ohio as though I don't even exist. I might come from a simple place but I'm not a simple person. I'm no fool."

"You need to trust him." The demand in Bobby's voice felt like a prickly cactus running across Jules's already too fragile emotional state.

"The only thing I need to do is take care of Frankie and get my life back together without Michael. I was foolish to think this was what he really wanted in his life. I'm sure if it weren't for the baby he'd have left months ago. How could a man like him ever settle for this?" Jules motioned around the tiny room as though nothing in it would be worthy of Michael's standards.

"Jules, Michael loves you and Frankie more than anything in this world. I don't know why he left like he did without saying anything to you. Maybe he was distraught. He just lost his dad." Piper's overly soft voice was as grating as Bobby's insistent one.

"Do not make excuses for him. There is nothing that makes leaving like that acceptable. It's been three full days, and I haven't heard a word from him. Not a single

4

word. Message received. It's time for me to pick up the pieces and realize Michael has something in Ohio I know nothing about and I have no interest in finding out what it is."

"Oh please," Bobby huffed with a roll of his eyes. "You can act as tough as you want, but we all know you're going to hunt him down and demand answers. That's how you work. You aren't going to just sit here and wait."

"You're damn right I'm not going to sit here and wait. I'm going to get on with my life and figure out what the hell we're going to do. I'm going to pack our stuff at Michael's apartment and move Frankie and me back in here. I'll get a job and take care of my child."

"No you won't," Bobby scoffed, and his arrogance pushed Jules to want to strike him across the face just to get a reprieve from his words. "I've known you a long time. I know you can't help yourself. You're going to go kick in doors until you get answers. You fight for what you want."

"Bobby, you knew me as a child. I'm not a child anymore. I'm a mother, and that changes everything. She is the only thing in my life that matters now." Jules gestured down at the crystal blue eyes of her daughter that were mirror images of Michael's, and it tore at her heart. "I will not act like a petulant child or a scorned woman. I'm a mother. I'm her mother. That's the only way I'll act. Michael made his choice to take off, and I made my choice to ignore the truth right in front of me. I can't change either of those things. But I can choose what I do next."

"You're going to find that man," Betty said flatly as she stepped into the doorway of the sitting room and folded her arms across her chest in that way that punctuated an argument.

"Ma, please don't. You of all people should understand what it means to put your child first. I'm not leaving her here just so I can go chase someone who clearly doesn't want me there."

"Did you want Michael to come after you when you took off like a mad woman to New York with Piper?"

"This is different."

"Yes it is, but don't leapfrog yourself here, child. Don't jump to the conclusion that Michael doesn't need you. I don't know his reasons and I don't agree with the way he did it, but I've had a good look at his heart and it's not capable of the things spinning in your head right now. If you're worried about your daughter and you're trying to give her the best life possible then go find her daddy and help him. Because I believe he needs you, even if he thinks he doesn't. "

Jules choked back the tears she'd been fighting since Michael left. She promised herself she wouldn't waste a minute crying over this, but her mother's words were shoving her toward the edge of losing that battle. "Ma, I just don't want to leave her right now. I don't want both Michael and me to be gone. I don't want her to think we abandoned her." And with that thought clamping down on her heart the tears began to fall. "She needs me."

"She needs both of you," Betty insisted, though her tone was softer. "He's gone after you before. He's shown up when you needed him to. Do the same for him."

"And if I get out there and don't like the answers I find? If he's not the man I thought he was?"

"Then you'll never have to ask yourself again if you are making the right choices for your daughter. You'll never have to wonder if digging your heels in and being angry hurt her more than helped her. If you face this now you'll be able to move forward knowing you are doing right by her, either way."

"I still don't want to leave her," Jules croaked as she slid off the couch and lay on the floor next to her cooing baby girl.

"I'll go with you," Piper said so quickly and loudly that Jules jumped slightly. "Frankie can come and I'll watch her while you sort things out. I'll be right there with you and so will she."

"Wait," Bobby cut in with a wave of his hands as though this situation had just spun out of control. "I can't come. I don't have any time off work, and I'm not sure it's a great idea for the three of you to go out there on your own since you don't know what's going on with Michael. With our track record it could be anything. I'm not comfortable with this."

"Well get comfortable, boy," Betty said with a threatening grin. "You ain't the boss of these girls, and if they want to go, you know damn well they'll go. I think you should save your breath."

"We'll be fine," Piper assured Bobby as she crossed the room and sat next to him. Normally she'd slide her hand into his, but Jules had begun noticing they weren't touching nearly as much since Michael left—as though their happiness contrasted too starkly with her agony.

"You're talking about the three most important people in my life hopping on a plane and walking into something we know nothing about. I'm not going to be able to get right with that. We need some other solution. Someone else needs to go too. Someone we trust. Someone competent."

"I'm sorry, are you implying we aren't trustworthy or competent?" Jules bit back, channeling all the anger she'd been bottling up.

"You're clouded by emotion and Piper will be focused on Frankie. If something is going on out there you'll both be distracted."

"Well, Jedda, Crystal, and Clay are busy at the restaurant. Willow and Josh are in New York, so who exactly did you have in mind?" Piper's question was almost as infuriating as Bobby's inference of their incompetence because she was entertaining the idea that he was right.

"What about my partner, Lindsey? She's on leave from work right now. She hurt her leg in a foot pursuit and I think she has two more weeks before she goes back on duty. I can ask her. I'm sure she's bored out of her mind right now. If we put her up in a hotel for a few days I'm sure she'd keep an eye on you."

"Could you stop talking like we're silly little girls who haven't ever done anything in their lives? We did just fine in New York by ourselves," Jules reminded him with a raised, attitude-laden eyebrow.

"Yes, right up until the point you almost got yourselves robbed and killed in an alley."

"Go to hell," Jules shouted as she kicked her foot at Bobby's shin and her tears turned to angry ones. "We don't need your hot little partner coming with us."

"She's not hot," Bobby said with a light kick back at her, like two children arguing over a toy. "She's like one of the guys and maybe if you weren't taking Frankie I wouldn't even bring it up, but Piper won't be able to be there for both of you. At least if you need help with something there will be an extra person out there.

"She is hot," Piper snickered with a bump of her elbow to Bobby's ribs. "But I actually agree with you this time. It might not hurt to have someone else with us. This way, if I have to bail you out of jail for kicking Michael's ass, the baby won't have to come with me."

The plausibility of that scenario was enough to open a crack in Jules's hardened stance. She wanted Frankie with her, but she knew there might be moments she'd want to shield her. Having someone else there, someone they trusted, could come in handy. "Fine," she acquiesced as she handed Frankie the toy she was reaching for.

"Now we just have to figure out where exactly Michael is. I'll be honest I don't know much about his family in Ohio or where exactly he'd have gone." Bobby leaned back on the couch and pulled out his phone. After typing in a few things he grimaced. "There are a lot of Coopers in Ohio. We'll need to narrow this down somehow. What else do you know, Jules?"

"Next to nothing." Jules shrugged, still angry with herself for being so blindly in love she'd ignored her own instincts about something being wrong. "But I know Michael and his father have the same name. He never uses the title, but I saw on some paperwork that he's Michael Joseph Cooper, Jr., so his father must be Senior.

Bobby typed again and his already downturned mouth drew even lower. "I found his father. The family lives in Cincinnati. Shit," he mouthed.

"What?" Jules asked shooting upright then sitting back down on the couch. "What is it? Just tell me."

"His father was a senator for eight years. Then became a lobbyist and philanthropist. The family is . . ."

"Is what?"

"Loaded. Like mansion and sports cars rich. His mother's name is Tabitha and his sister is Josephine." Bobby spun the phone so Jules could see the photo from the newspaper article written about the untimely death of such a great man.

Jules lost her breath for a moment as she stared at the pictures. There were three. One was of a man who looked so similar to Michael, just older, that it made her want to cry again. She couldn't tell if it was because she so desperately missed Michael's face or if it was knowing this man was dead now. The second picture was of Michael's mother and father standing in front of an enormous white house with a pillared porch and glossy front steps. Between them was the sweetest looking young woman with rosy cheeks in a gorgeous floral dress. This was Michael's little sister, Josephine. She favored her mother, both of them with long, blond hair full of carefully sculpted waves, meant to look effortless but clearly taking time to create so beautifully. Their eyes were bright emeralds that lit up their whole face. The joy that came through in this picture made Jules ache for their loss and wonder why Michael had kept them from her. They looked like perfectly wonderful people.

Then as she looked at the third picture it all became clear. She looked at the picture of a much younger Michael, his hair longer and his face thinner, his body lacking the muscle he carried with him today. There he stood, his father's arm around him as they leaned on a brand new cherry-red car that probably cost more than the house they were sitting in front of and all the cars in the driveway combined. The smile on Michael's face was so large and the pride in his father's eyes so apparent. Behind them was another angle of their sprawling and

10

gorgeously landscaped home. Their clothes were pristine and designer. They were wealthy, likely incredibly so. It was clear now. There was nothing wrong with these people, no reason to hide them from her. It was her he was hiding. She didn't fit at all into the world she was seeing in these pictures. He'd never want to bring someone like her home to a family of such prominence.

"Maybe we shouldn't go," she said, sucking in a deep breath. "It looks like the life he has out there doesn't really go with the life I have. He must be embarrassed by me."

"Shut your mouth," Betty cut in as she tossed the dishtowel at Jules. "You are the best thing that ever happened to that man. If that's the reason he's been keeping you separate from his past then go find out and realize he's a fool. But know there ain't no amount of money in the world can make a bad person good. If you've got an ugly heart you can't buy a new one. But a good person is worth his weight in gold. You're plenty good enough for him and his family."

"I'm sure that's not it, Jules," Piper said, reaching across Bobby and taking Jules's hand. "We'll get to the bottom of it."

Frankie let out a cry Jules knew meant she was hungry, and though she was exhausted she stood up and lifted the baby to her hip. "I've got to feed her." She stepped out of the room and heard a set of footsteps behind her.

"Let me hold her while you make something," Bobby said as he opened his arms to the baby who gladly reached out to be received.

"Thanks," Jules said, handing the baby over. "But I think I should get used to doing it on my own. I might be alone from now on."

Bobby kissed the top of Frankie's head and then pulled Jules to him, planting an identical kiss through her mop of messy red hair. "No matter what you find there, you will never be in this alone. I love you, and I love this baby. I'm sorry you're going through this, but don't for a second worry that you'll have to fly solo. You and Frankie will always have me."

While his words brought her comfort, nothing could fill the cavernous sinkhole of fear that opened up the moment Michael left. She didn't want to live a single day without her husband. She didn't want her daughter to suffer the same fate she had and have to live for even a moment without her father. Bobby was a loyal and proven friend whom she loved dearly, but nothing would replace her husband. And no matter how tough she was trying to act, that reality was too powerful to ignore. She needed Michael.

Chapter Two

Michael rolled the paper program in his hand over and over again as he wondered how many people in the room could decipher the lies from the truth regarding his late father. Friends and acquaintances strode up to the podium at his father's funeral and, with somber faces, told stories of the man's generosity, his brilliant business mind, and his loyalty. When someone died it wasn't uncommon for him to become saint-like in the eyes of the living, but surely his father was so far from that for anyone to take this seriously. Michael wondered if they were fools or just as good at being despicable liars as his father was.

Though he was nearly drowning under his callus feelings, he could already see himself slipping back into his family's world. He'd shaken a thousand hands, accepted condolences, and acted as though he gave a shit about the bastard in the casket at the front of the church right now. Like an actor transforming into an old familiar part, he was following the script laid out before him. It all came back to him like water over a dam the moment he'd seen his mother. She was always perfectly polished. Her designer dress and styled hair, the glimmering jewelry, and today, the black pillbox hat with a small veil covering half her face. Being back in her glamorous presence turned him back into the person she taught him to be. Fake.

As the last person stepped away from the microphone, his mother's threatening glare forced him to go up. He'd told her at least ten times he didn't want to speak. He'd let her decide what story she would spin to explain away his silence. She could blame it on

13

overwhelming grief or laryngitis for all he cared. But like usual, in the presence of a crowd, she'd ignored what Michael said and put him on the spot. Every weepy eye in this church was focused on him now, and though his brain was filled with blazing curse words, his legs still carried him obediently to the podium.

"Thank you all so much for gathering here with us today," Michael croaked out as he worked to find his voice. Closing his eyes for a moment, his mind wandered to the courtroom, the place he always felt comfortable speaking, and he tried to channel that. "I see so many familiar faces along with some new ones." Scanning the room he took stock of how ridiculous all of this was. He spotted a former business partner who'd been sold out by his father and ended up serving two years in prison as a result. There were two former secretaries who had turned quickly into mistresses. The years hadn't been great to either of them and his father would likely not give them a second look were he alive today. "What can I say about my father?" Michael began slowly, hoping someone might stand up and give him that answer.

What special memories did he have of his father? There were no games of catch in the yard to speak of. Michael couldn't think of a single time his father had attended any of his hockey practices. So like a good Cooper, he lied. "My father and I traveled frequently together. One trip to Paris in particular always resonates with me. As we ate at a little café my father began speaking to a waiter named Mel. He was a young kid with tired eyes who was covering a couple dozen tables like a pro. Mel was nineteen; he'd lost his parents in a car accident the previous summer and was now helping to care for his two younger siblings. He was determined to

14

keep them all together. My father listened intently to this story and made sure Mel knew how impressed he was with not only his good intentions but how professional he was. When our meal was over my father pulled a roll of bills from his pocket and laid the equivalent of one thousand US dollars on the table. On the back of his business card he wrote a note. *If you would like to contact me I would be happy to interview you for a job with one of my Parisian partners.*

"I remember sitting there thinking how much this would change Mel's life and how my father had done this without a second thought. He saw someone who deserved a chance, and he didn't hesitate to offer it to him. That's how I choose to remember my father," Michael said as he took in a deep breath and lowered his head as though he were gathering himself. In truth, he was trying to swallow down the true version of that story. Mel was actually Melanie. The scenario with her parents was the same but the job his father was offering her was far less admirable than how Michael had portrayed it in his story. Later on that trip to Paris he would see Melanie sneaking out of his father's hotel room, her clothes disheveled and her hair a mess. Nothing about the note his father had left had been rooted in generosity. His father did nothing without getting something in return. But that story wouldn't have set well with the mourning crowd.

Michael stepped down from the podium feeling as though he was caging a scream and, at any moment, it would break free. He moved past his seat and went right for the door of the church, knowing if he didn't get some fresh air in his lungs he'd burst. When he pushed the heavy wooden door with the stained glassed window open he felt like he'd just come up too fast from a scuba dive. His head was spinning and the pain in his chest was shockingly sharp. He moved around the side of the church to a bench in a clearing near statues of playing children.

"A hard day isn't it, son," Father Diplin asked as he walked up behind Michael, scaring him half to death. He'd been the family's priest for as long as Michael could remember, and back before everything Michael believed in was destroyed, he'd had great admiration for the church and Father Diplin.

"Sorry I stepped out, Father, I just needed some air."

"Who wouldn't on a day like today? Burying your father is never easy," he offered as he took a seat on the bench next to Michael and adjusted his white collar slightly.

"Yes, it's hard to sit in there." Michael didn't finish that sentence by admitting the hypocrisy in the church had him fleeing for fresh air. He couldn't meet the priest's eyes, so he stared down at the shoes his mother had left out for him this morning. From the corner of his eye he could still see the white beard and big gold-rimmed glasses of the man who didn't seem to be leaving.

"I'd imagine it's hard to look at all those people and not want to scream the truth. If they all knew the real man your father was, do you think there would be so many people in there today?" Father Diplin's warm and level voice shot through Michael like a lightning bolt, drawing his gaze right back to the man's face so their eyes were locked on each other. "I'm not blind, son, nor am I deaf. I took your father's confession once a month for the last twenty years. I likely know more about what he's done than you do. I am a man of God, and I have a responsibility to his flock. Your father was a member of this church and my duty was to guide and support him. But if I had been in your position," he hesitated as he squeezed down on Michael's shoulder, "I'd have run for the hills, too. You may not know it but I've kept up on your story. You're living in a little town practicing law now and really helping people. You're the honorable man here today. I know that. God knows that, too. It's admirable that you've come back to pay your respects and care for your mother, but listen to me closely, son, the first chance you get, go back to your life. There is nothing here for a man like you."

All Michael could muster was a nod of his head and a blink of his wide and shocked eyes. The priest stood, a little spring in his step and a casual whistle on his lips, and headed back toward the entrance of the church. The validation he'd just given Michael was greater then any condolence or fake sympathy anyone had offered him since he'd arrived. Now all he had to do was take the wise man's advice and be ready to get the hell out of here as soon as he could.

Chapter Three

"Lindsey, it's so nice of you to come with us," Piper said, obviously trying to compensate for Jules's silence. They'd all been quiet on the car ride to the airport and throughout the entire flight, and now as they rode silently in the rental car headed for the hotel; Piper clearly couldn't take it anymore. Jules, on the other hand, didn't care if any of them ever said a word for the remainder of this trip. She was too busy trying to remind herself how much she'd miss if she went to jail for murdering her husband.

"It's no problem at all. I was going out of my mind being on leave. My knee is completely healed, but they won't clear me for another week or so. I've never been to Ohio so I'm looking forward to it." Lindsey's long blond hair was down, something Jules had never seen before. She had a bit of makeup on, though she didn't need it. Rather than workout clothes or her uniform she was in jeans and a thin sage-green sweater. She looked like a real human being, not Bobby's partner.

"Well this isn't a vacation or anything," Jules snapped out, knowing her attitude was misplaced but unable to contain it. "I am trying to confront my husband, who has kept his entire family a secret from me and I'm guessing I'm a secret to them. I don't know why, but I'm assuming it's not going to have a happy ending either way. So I'd be ready with your handcuffs or bail money."

Lindsey let out a loud laugh and then stopped abruptly when she realized neither of the other women were laughing. "Listen, Jules, whatever happens here I'll help you out. Short of hiding a body, I'll do what I can for you. I'm a great babysitter if you need that. Or I'm a

18

pretty good freelance detective if you want me hunting information down. Just," Lindsey turned toward Jules and with a half smile and warm eyes spoke kindly, "don't be a bitch to me. I get enough flack at work every day for being a woman. I've got guys treating me like dirt on a regular basis. I'm looking forward to a week away where people actually remember I'm a human being."

Jules felt like she'd just gotten punched in the stomach. She'd forgotten how hard it must be for a woman to be on the police force in a place like Edenville. Lindsey was here doing them a favor and she deserved better. "Sorry about that," Jules murmured. "I appreciate you being here. I'm on edge and feel like lashing out. I'll save it for Michael though."

"And if you're really nice to me I might change my mind about hiding the body." Lindsey laughed, and now Piper joined in. The most Jules could muster was a half smile as she popped a pacifier into Frankie's mouth.

"So what's our plan?" Lindsey asked as the GPS chimed they were arriving at the hotel.

"There is an event tonight, some kind of gala celebrating Michael's father's life. I'm going to go. I want to see him face to face. He won't be able to lie if I'm looking him right in the eyes."

"I'll go with you," Lindsey said, not posing it as a question at all. "Piper can stay with Frankie tonight since the baby is more comfortable with her."

"I think I should go," Piper cut in. "I know Michael and maybe seeing both of us will be impactful for him."

"What's your plan when Jules loses her mind and starts dumping punch bowls on people? How are you going to contain the scene?" Lindsey asked, scrutinizing

Piper's face. Jules looked back and forth between both women and spoke before Piper could.

"She's right. You might be too close to the situation to help me if I really lose it. Plus Frankie *is* more comfortable with you. You know her routine. But, Lindsey, this gala is five hundred dollars a plate. It's a fundraiser for one of the family's charities and it's black tie. I brought a dress but what will you wear?"

"Well I don't have a black tie," Lindsey shrugged, "but I'll make do. Just let me know what time to meet you in the lobby of the hotel and I'll be there with bells on."

As they walked through the parking lot of the hotel, Jules worried if Lindsey would truly have some kind of outfit with bells on it. The only thing that mattered tonight was finding and confronting Michael. But part of her was terrified Michael was embarrassed about Jules's humble origins. Walking in with an underdressed Lindsey would only make the gap between her lifestyle and that of the Coopers even more glaring.

Chapter Four

Michael straightened the bow tie of his tuxedo and pulled on each of the sleeves to get it perfectly positioned. The funeral was over and all that was left was a gala celebrating his father's generosity. It was laughable, really. He took a swig of the gin he'd bought in a flask. It barely put a dent in his ragged nerves but something was better than nothing.

As he walked down one of the many long, shimmering clean hallways of his parents' house, back toward the entryway, he heard his mother's falsely warm voice.

"Michael dear, may I speak with you for a moment?" She was dressed in a gorgeous black flowing gown embellished with crystals and lace. Like always, the neckline scooped just low enough to still be deemed respectable but showed his mother was not shy about her mostly paid for body.

"Yes, Mother?" Michael asked, not trying to hide his reluctance as he turned toward her.

"It means the world to me that you are here for us, Michael," she hummed as she reached up and touched his cheek affectionately. "Your sister and I need you so much right now. I've been waiting for the right moment to talk to you about this. Do you think you and I can sit down after lunch tomorrow?"

"I'll be gone by then, Mother." Michael's tone was flat and unwavering. He had no intention of getting sucked into spending more time here. He needed to be back with Jules and Frankie in Edenville before it was too late to earn his wife's forgiveness.

"You mustn't leave, Michael. We need you here. You, more than anyone in the world, understand how disastrous it would be if your father's company were taken over by anyone outside the family. Your sister and I aren't prepared to handle what needs to be done. You need to step in and take control of your father's business and his charities."

"There is no chance in hell I'm associating myself with his business or his charities. They are a sham. He's extorted and embezzled more money than he's ever donated. Why in the world would I walk into that?" The snap in Michael's voice was partially driven by the slight buzz he was feeling, but his answer would be the same sober. He'd left this place as a twenty-four-year-old with absolutely no intention of ever associating his name with the criminal activities taking place.

"You don't have to agree with your father's business practices, but I thought you'd at least care enough about your sister and me to try to protect us from the backlash that will come if any of those things are exposed. Our family would be ruined. The charities we have that do good in this world would be dissolved. The people we help would all go without. Not to mention all the people your father's manufacturing company employees. This is bigger than just your moral high ground, Michael." Her voice was a low whisper with a hiss in it that reminded Michael of who she really was.

"My moral high ground has never been enough to protect any of us. That's why I left. That's the only thing that works—distance. You were by no means ignorant of the business decisions, Mother. You played an active role in flat-out stealing people's money. I'm not going to put myself between you and that bullet. You chose Dad; you chose to stay with him and be his partner in all this. I'm sorry he died and left you holding the bag, but that isn't my problem. I'm going to this gala tonight, and I'm leaving after breakfast tomorrow. That's final." Michael's voice boomed and echoed through the large entryway as he stormed out of the house and leaned against one of the pillars that stood like soldiers guarding their front door.

"Hey stranger," his sister's voice called through a smile. "I feel like we haven't even had a chance to talk yet." She was wearing a short, black, form-fitting dress with a necklace so full of diamonds it hurt his eyes when it caught the light of the sun.

He opened his arms to her and she dove in for a hug. She was still so small. She was born premature and Michael remembered how frightened he was that she might not survive. He was twelve years old, and he swore if she lived he'd donate his entire comic book collection to charity. The day she came home from the hospital he boxed them up and had the chauffer drive him to Goodwill. It was a deal he was still so glad he made.

"Sorry we haven't really talked yet, Jo," he said, kissing the top of her head. He released her and watched as she flattened out her dress and adjusted her necklace, exactly the way their mother would have. She resembled her more than he'd ever realized, and his only hope was that their similarities stopped at appearances. But it soon became clear that wasn't the case.

"Please don't call me Jo. My name is Josephine. It's impossible to be taken seriously when people call you Jo. Mother says you're finally staying in town to take over Dad's company and his charities. I want to talk to you about that."

Michael never wanted to be sharp with his sister. He felt bad for her, really. She still idolized their parents and was completely ignorant to all the things Michael had discovered about them. Dozens of times when they argued about Michael leaving town and not coming back, he considered telling her the truth. But in the end he always decided not to rob her of the illusion that she was in the presence of great people. There were days he wished he'd never been robbed of it himself.

"Mother was wrong. I'm not staying, Jo." He knew she didn't want to be called that but he didn't want to feed into the idea that she was anything other than the kid he left behind here years ago.

"You're running again? Seriously? Our father just died. He's left behind an enormous amount of unfinished business and you don't care. Mother just lost her husband. Don't you think she could use you for support?" There was a determination in her eyes that instantly reminded Michael of his mother when she became dead set on getting her way. Suddenly all he could feel was sadness.

If Jo knew anything about their parents' relationship she'd realize, as Michael did, that there was no love lost between them. The death of her husband was probably a welcomed relief to Tabitha—outside of the business troubles he was leaving behind, that is. "Why don't you come with me Jo? I have a great life back East. You could be happy there, just like I am."

"You're a moron. You don't know anything about me or what makes me happy. Stop calling me Jo. I'm not a child. I graduated summa cum laude. I could take any one of a hundred jobs I've been offered around the country but I have a life here. I'm engaged, which you'd

24

know if you'd acted like my brother at all in the last decade. I'll be married here, and I don't plan to abandon our mother even if you've found a way to live with yourself for doing it."

"You don't understand. When I leave, things are going to come out about Dad. You're going to hear things that you aren't expecting." Michael felt himself stepping farther onto thin ice.

She shot up her hand to quiet him. "Enough with all of this, Michael. I know you and Dad never got along. He expected a lot from you and when things got tough you left. I know he was hard on you, but guess what? He's dead. You have nothing left to fight against here. So don't project your relationship with him onto me. He was different with me. Older and kinder by the time I was growing up. I'm sorry you didn't get to see that part of him, but maybe if you hadn't left you would have given him a chance to change with you.

Her words didn't even dent the armor he'd wrapped himself in. She was naive and ignorant to who he was. His relationship with his father wasn't a complicated one. It was incredibly straightforward. Michael was groomed to be a part of his empire and when he got a peek behind the curtain at the smoke and mirrors, he'd left. "Congratulations on your engagement," Michael conceded as he lifted his sister's hand and looked down at the enormous ring on her finger. It was double the size of the diamond he'd given to Jules and surrounded by a dozen smaller diamonds.

"Thank you," she replied, the snap in her voice waning. "Our engagement party is this weekend. It would mean a lot to me if you would stay long enough to celebrate with Wilson and me. He's in the middle of law school himself. Dad was really pushing him along, hoping he'd be a part of the family business some day."

Michael had to swallow back the venom he was tempted to shoot out across the yard. Of course his father was pushing the boy along. It's what he'd done to him too. He'd encouraged him to go into law and opened every door possible for him. What Michael didn't know was that he was grooming him to be his own personal lawyer. Someone who could cut corners and cover up all the things he needed in order to continue stealing and lying. If he hadn't died he likely would have succeeded in pulling in Jo's poor new fiancé.

"I can't stay for the party Jo—Josephine. I wish I could but I've got to get back East. But we have tonight. Do you want to head over to the gala together like we used to?"

"No, Michael, I don't, because I have a life and a fiancé who I'll be going with. I'm not busy hiding away from the world like a hermit. You can go alone, and stay alone the rest of your life for all I care," she shouted with a quiver in her voice that told Michael she still cared very much. She stormed out to a waiting car and slammed her door tightly.

As much as he wanted to save his sister from the media storm of truths that would come in the wake of their father's death, he knew you couldn't force people to protect themselves. Jo was right. She wasn't a child anymore. If this were where she wanted to place her allegiance then she'd need to find a place to stand when everything came crashing down about their father. When she learned of the stealing and the affairs, she'd need to be that adult she was claiming to be. If they began seizing assets and freezing bank accounts Jo would need to be

Josephine and live with her own choices. That was easy to say, but at the end of the day she was still his baby sister. Becoming a father had put so much of Michael's life into perspective and a part of him wanted to rescue Jo. But not more than he needed to save his marriage and protect Jules and Frankie from this world. And that meant getting home to them as soon as possible.

Chapter Five

With tearful eyes, Jules put her favorite lipstick on. She couldn't believe she hadn't worn any since before she'd had Frankie. It had been seven months without any makeup, really. She could barely face herself in the mirror now as she began to transform from tired mom to elegant gala attendee.

Maybe the fact there was a transformation at all had contributed to Michael's leaving. Being a mother had changed her so deeply perhaps he didn't recognize or love the woman she was today. Maybe that's what made it so easy for him to keep secrets and leave without her.

Honestly, she didn't always like what she saw in the mirror most days either. Though she didn't remember it happening, the majority of her days were spent in yoga pants and dirty oversized shirts. She'd become so used to the smell of spit-up from her colicky baby she'd stopped making sure it was at least out of her hair by the time Michael got home from work. Her makeup was all stashed away and hardly used. She hadn't dried her hair straight or even attempted to try on any of her pre-pregnancy clothes. Even though she was only about five pounds over her original weight she could tell her body had changed dramatically. Her hips would never be able to wiggle their way back into her old jeans. Her boobs were too big for all her shirts, and not in a sexy way, just in an engorged with milk kind of way.

How could she expect a man like Michael, who came from such wealth and prestige, to tough it out through a time when she didn't feel very tough at all? This was all supposed to be different. She was supposed to be joyful. Loving Frankie was effortless. It was a deep and protective love Jules felt the instant she held her child. But the day-to-day was not filled with that constant bond.

Managing her time was now impossible. How could a day go by so painfully slow but at the same time so fast that she'd accomplished next to nothing. She was always playing catch-up. She'd wash, dry, and iron just enough clothes for Michael to go to work the next day. The dishes she managed to wash would be enough to eat on that night. How was she always down to just one clean pacifier and burp cloth? When Michael came home and stumbled over Frankie's tummy-time mat, Jules would feel crushed inside. How had she not picked that up? Wasn't that what Michael would be thinking?

It didn't make any sense, really. She'd run an office for years with seventeen employees. She had a vast amount of responsibility and bi-annual audits that were high stakes. Maybe that was the point, though. Twice a year someone would come in, scrutinize her work, and tell her what she needed to improve. But she'd also hear what she was excelling at. Now, as a mother, she lacked any kind of score. Where was the grade that told her what she was doing well and what she needed to work on? Couldn't someone come in and shadow her for a day and give her some kind of number that told what her worth was? Because without it she was feeling worthless.

In the middle of the night, rocking away as she fed Frankie, she knew she was supposed to feel pride in her ability to give her child sustenance and life. But Frankie hardly ever slept, which meant Jules didn't either. So all she felt in those moments was drained—physically and emotionally tapped out. Some days her only friend was the rhythmic chattering sound of the breast pump, which

Jules swore sounded like "go to sleep, go to sleep, go to sleep."

The need for the pump at all was something that brought her immense guilt. She should have been able to nurse her baby but the two of them could never quite get in sync. The pump had become the best solution for them but it frequently made Jules feel like a failure.

It wouldn't be crazy to think she could talk to her mother about this. Surely she'd be empathetic. The same would go for Piper or even Michael. But the only thing more frightening than thinking you are failing as a mother, is knowing other people are thinking the same thing. So she cried her tears at night, alone in the bathroom.

She was exhausted knowing not only her *wants* but her *needs* now fell second. It was hard to understand how you could no longer be a priority in your own life. Need to go to the bathroom: too bad, the baby is hungry. Sleep deprived to the point of nausea: oh well, the baby is wide awake and wants your attention. The weight of that on her was heavy. Then the guilt over the weight felt even heavier.

Maybe Michael was feeling the same way. Perhaps the nagging thoughts of regret and the stark changes to their lifestyle had become too much for him. Had she become too much of a mom and stopped being enough wife for him? Or worse, maybe he didn't feel tired or regretful at all, but maybe he could tell she did and that was enough to drive him away.

She stepped into the dark navy dress she'd borrowed from the seamstress back in Edenville when they found out about the gala. She looked in the mirror and realized how perfectly it fit her, how amazing she felt when she was this dressed up and put together. Then from the other side of the door she heard Frankie crying and she was instantly wracked with guilt for leaving her daughter tonight.

"Hey Jules, are you almost ready? Lindsey is already downstairs," Piper called through the door as Jules dried her tears. Her life could be on the brink of a dramatic change tonight, and though she was struggling to pinpoint what caused it, she knew she had to face it either way.

Drawing in a deep breath she stepped out of the bathroom and reached for her daughter, but Piper leaned away, keeping Frankie in her arms. "She just took a bottle, she'll spit up on your dress."

Jules leaned in and kissed her daughter on her pudgy cheek and sucked in a long whiff of her powdery scent.

"You know her schedule, right?" Jules asked, opening up the diaper bag again and making sure everything was there.

"We'll be fine. You just take care of what you need to tonight and know that no matter what happens I'll be here for you and Frankie. So will Bobby." Piper patted Frankie on the back, and Jules fought the urge to show her a better way to get the baby to burp. It was only one night away from her daughter, and it was for something important.

After stepping out of the elevator and into the lobby, Jules prayed Lindsey would be dressed in something mildly elegant so they wouldn't stick out like a sore thumb at the gala. She was convinced they'd be the only two with a southern drawl; they didn't need to look the part of farm folk too.

"There you are," Lindsey huffed as she touched Jules's elbow, sending her jumping almost out of her high heels. Jules couldn't believe her eyes as she took in the vision that was Lindsey. In a stunning long chiffon dress that hugged her usually hidden curves and a side slit that ran the length of nearly all her leg, Lindsey looked incredible. Her hair had been curled and looked as though volume had been magically injected right into it at the roots. With masterfully applied smoky eye makeup she looked like a runway model.

"Lindsey, you look amazing," Jules stuttered, taking a step back to get another perspective.

"I went down to the shopping area and picked up this dress. I'm keeping the tags on it so I can take it back tomorrow," she whispered as she leaned in. It reminded Jules of a saying of her mother's: *You can dress up a circus monkey but you can't change her ways.* Jules was feeling a lot like a circus monkey herself trying to walk in heels instead of sneakers like she had been doing for almost a year.

They hopped in a town car Jules had hired because the rental car wouldn't cut it and a cab was too low class for this type of event. As they gave the address to the driver they saw a smile spread across his unshaven face. "I don't need directions, ladies. I know where that event is tonight. Everyone does."

Jules and Lindsey exchanged a half-annoyed look as they sat back in the car. Jules readied herself for any possibility this evening. Would she find Michael with another woman? Maybe a whole other family? Or was he trying to keep her hidden from his mother and sister because he was embarrassed by her? Maybe becoming a parent so quickly was something he couldn't deal with; maybe it had changed his life and he was looking for an out.

As the car weaved its way down the street, Jules took note of the changing landscape. The farther they were from their economy hotel, the larger and more opulent the houses became. The driveways seemed to stretch endlessly and the houses, though grand and stately, appeared far less approachable and welcoming. The line that separated the common person from the wealthy grew wider. Jules couldn't even picture Michael on the other side of that line. Sure, he was polished and educated, but wasn't this the same man who sat next to her on Sunday afternoons binge-watching terrible television shows in his sweatpants? Nothing about any of this felt right.

Chapter Six

As a child Michael hated galas and events because they stole his parents away from him. Not just for the evening, either. His mother, if charged with planning, would be off choosing fabric swatches and sampling entrées for months before an event. Her life objective became topping the last event she attended. That summed her up perfectly, really. An event like this was the culmination of hours of work to create an illusion of perfection. But behind the large midnight blue curtains that draped every wall of the gala venue, there were inevitable dents and gouges. Under the crisp white tablecloths, the tables were worn by the years.

Michael downed his second glass of champagne as he scanned the room again. The doors had just opened, and the people were swarming in like locusts. The chatter was all rolling together like a buzzing alarm through Michael's aching head. He wanted to punch a wall. He wanted to be holding his daughter and begging his wife to understand why he'd left and not answered her calls. He wanted to be anywhere but here.

"Michael," he heard his mother chirp as she squeezed the back of his arm, an indication that she had something that required his attention. "I know you haven't had a chance to speak with Elizabeth. Now seems the perfect time." Her words cut through him, and he took a long moment before turning around to face his mother and the woman he'd been avoiding since he'd returned to Ohio.

"Hello Elizabeth," he said with the slightest sign of a smile, all he could muster. Her smile, on the other hand, was enormous. She hadn't changed much since the last

34

time Michael had seen her, though this time she wasn't crying and begging him not to leave. Her eyes were still the darkest brown he'd ever seen but now, rather than their natural glow, they were surrounded with so much makeup you could hardly see how naturally beautiful they were.

"I missed you at the services. I thought maybe you were trying to avoid me." Elizabeth's voice was sultry as she brushed her hand against Michael's shoulder teasingly.

"I'll leave you two to catch up," his mother chimed with a waggle of her eyebrows. "Oh do you hear that? Isn't that your song the orchestra is playing? I could really use someone to break the ice on the dance floor. Thank you for volunteering." His mom shooed them both toward the floor, and Elizabeth practically jumped into Michael's reluctant arms.

"It's been so long, but you still look great," Elizabeth cooed as she peered affectionately up into Michael's eyes. "It's been a hell of a year for me. I just signed my divorce papers."

"I'm sorry to hear it didn't work out with you and Mark," Michael offered, averting his eyes and focusing on making sure for every centimeter Elizabeth moved in he moved an equal distance away.

"He is engaged to his mistress now. It's ridiculous. She's nineteen years old. I swear if it weren't for the colossal alimony I'd want to kill him. There are rules and he broke them."

"I'm sorry he cheated on you. Wedding vows aren't meant to be ignored like that."

"I'm not naïve, Michael. Every man is going to cheat. That's just a given. The rules I'm talking about are discretion, and if you are exposed you don't go out and marry the little twit. It's mortifying."

Any bit of nostalgic warmth for the girl he'd deserted here years ago was instantly extinguished by the realization she'd become one of them. Elizabeth was no different than his mother or any of the other myopic and selfish women here tonight. They'd all traded their dignity for a fancy dress, a large bank account, and a glamorous house.

"It makes me wish things had worked out between you and me," Elizabeth said with a smile as she reached up and ran a hand through Michael's hair. The pit of his stomach flamed at the thought of his own marriage vows. "Maybe this timing is fate's way of telling us we should give it another try."

"How can you live like this, Elizabeth," Michael asked, jerking his head away from her hand. "You are better than just expecting a cheating husband and cashing in on alimony. You're better than this world."

"This world is what afforded you an education and funded your entire childhood. Every advantage you have comes from here. What's your problem?" Elizabeth's dark eyes narrowed and Michael knew she was contemplating whether or not he was one of them. If he weren't careful the entire conversation would change and the rumors she'd spread would take over this entire party quickly.

"I'm sorry." He shook his head as though he were fighting off a haunting ghost. "It's been an emotional time, that's all. I'm just overwhelmed."

"Of course," Elizabeth comforted as she squeezed his bicep. "I should have been more sensitive; I'm sorry. I was hoping maybe there would still be something between us."

"It's over," Michael said flatly as he released her and stepped backward. "The song, it's over. I'm going to grab another glass of champagne."

"I'll come with you," Elizabeth offered as she laced her arm in his and smiled at the chattering heads, who were eyeing them like paparazzi hunting a socialite.

"Michael," his sister called from the open terrace behind them. "Mother wants us to take some photos. She said to bring Elizabeth."

"I'm grabbing a drink," Michael groaned, trying to ignore his sister.

"Now, Michael," Jo insisted as she pointed toward the large garden below the terrace. "The newspaper is here and they want a shot of us."

"I'll stay with you, Michael." Elizabeth tightened her grip on his arm as she spun toward the door and led him away from the champagne.

He tried desperately to remind himself this was all temporary. By tomorrow night he'd be on a plane heading back to Edenville and trying to put his life back together. This toxic, all-consuming place would be just a blip on his radar, and he could go back to pretending it never existed.

Chapter Seven

"Are you sure you're ready?" Lindsey asked as she and Jules stared up at the large marble steps in front of them. There were droves of people heading through the large oak doors, held open by men in tuxedos. Everyone looked pristinely put together, and Jules immediately felt as though her lack of accessories would be spotted by every eye in the room. She didn't have the glamorous, shimmering diamond necklace or the boxy, embellished clutch tucked under the crook of her arm. "Bobby said Michael told him he'd be back in Edenville by the weekend. There is still time to turn around and just wait for Michael to come back."

"If I don't see what's going on with my own two eyes I'll never be able to let him just waltz back into town with an explanation and pretend that's enough for me. Going in there and facing whatever this is about is the only way I'm going to be able to move on or forgive him." Jules sucked in a deep breath and pulled the bottom of her long dress up slightly as she ascended the large steps toward the hall.

Stepping inside, she heard Lindsey let out an audible curse word that summed up exactly how Jules was feeling. The majesty of this room was breathtaking. The high ceilings were decorated with a million tiny globes of light, casting the most beautiful glow. The walls were draped in lush dark blue material, giving the illusion of being underwater. Jules had been one of those girls who, as a child, closed her eyes at night and wished she would magically wake up as a princess the next morning. She'd read every fashion magazine and dreamed about living a life like she saw on television. Edenville always seemed too small for her eclectic dynamic personality, but somehow she never left her hometown.

She knew her eyes were as large as saucers as she took in every tiny detail that all added up to picture-perfect beauty. The smell of expensive perfume and gourmet food almost bowled her over.

"Welcome, ladies," a man's voice called out behind them, sending them both jumping slightly. "I'm Spencer Clintensburg. I'll be your concierge for tonight's event. Anything you need, I'll ensure you have it." The pointy-nosed man in white gloves and a tuxedo passed them each a glass of champagne. "The caviar table is to your left; dinner will be served in just under an hour. The orchestra is taking requests and the silent auction begins at ten o'clock."

"Thank you," Jules muttered as she smiled warmly at the short man with a combover.

"May I introduce you around the room or are you familiar with many guests here tonight?" he asked, gesturing toward the crowd of people.

"We're friends with the Cooper family," Lindsey chimed in. "We've just flown in and were sorry to miss the services. We'd like to pay our condolences. Are they all here tonight?"

"They are. Mrs. Cooper," the man started and Jules had to bite her tongue from answering as though he was talking to her, since that was her name as well, "is always a very gracious host and will surely be on the floor making her rounds most of the night. Her daughter, Josephine, has been quiet since the passing of her father, but I'm sure she'll be out for the silent auction. The Coopers are public servants at heart, and they always rally for a cause. I've worked for the family for over a decade now."

"And Michael?" Jules asked, holding her breath until she heard the answer.

"Yes, he is here as well. I just saw him on the dance floor with his girlfriend, Elizabeth. I believe they stepped out back for some pictures for the newspaper."

"Elizabeth?" Jules coughed out over a sip of her champagne.

"Yes, a very sweet girl Michael has known since high school. It warmed my heart to see them out there dancing. I think they are an exceptional couple. Two well-pedigreed families coming together is never a bad thing." Spencer tipped his head and winked at the idea of the cute couple. "Can I get you anything else for now?"

"I'll take another glass of champagne," Jules demanded with her free hand, waving for another glass.

"You want two glasses of champagne?" Spencer asked, looking confused.

"No I want ten glasses," Jules barked, grabbing the second glass from the passing tray by herself. "But I only have two hands so that's going to have to do for now."

She turned on her heel and made her way toward the back of the room. The open doors to the terrace were blocked by gawking people, and she had every intention of knocking over as many as she could on her way out.

"Stop, Jules," Lindsey ordered and clutched the meat of her arm tightly. "Take a breath and let's make a plan here. You don't need to blow up on him right now in public. That's going to make you look like the bad guy."

"And what do you suggest? It better involve tossing these two glasses of champagne in his face."

40

"There are a dozen sides to every story, and right now you know one," Lindsey stressed as she took the two glasses gently from her. Jules could see Lindsey's expertise kicking in, like she was talking someone off a ledge with just the right amount of firmness and empathy. "Let me go out there and talk to him. You go off somewhere quiet, like over by the window, and I'll send him in."

Jules couldn't muster the words to agree, but she gave a nearly imperceptible nod that seemed enough for Lindsey. She made her way to the window and looked down over the expansive gardens that had been pruned into a work of art. She wished she were here for some other reason. She wished she had come to this event on Michael's arm and been able to experience it with an air of enthusiasm rather than the molten hot rage she was feeling.

Through the perfectly spotless window she finally spotted Michael in a sea of people. There were flashing cameras and hustling staff jogging around looking busy. And on her husband's arm was a staggeringly gorgeous woman whose diamonds sparkled brighter than the stars on a cloudless night in Edenville.

Though Jules had started the evening feeling pretty in her dress, the sight of this woman washed that away with the force of a tsunami. Her long brown hair cascaded over her toned shoulders in tight ringlets that looked like they'd taken all day to sculpt. Her smile was so perfect and glistening it seemed to cast a light around her. The gown she wore had an open back that plunged low and showcased her elegant and feminine back. But it was the way she was standing that struck Jules the hardest. This woman belonged here. She stood in a way that said she'd been to a thousand of these events.

Jules held her breath as Lindsey approached Michael. The way his face froze with shock pained her; he looked like he'd been caught as he hastily shook the gorgeous woman off his arm and stepped to the side to hear what Lindsey had to say. His gaze shifted toward the window where Jules stood, and he shook his head in disbelief before charging up the stairs in a near run.

When he burst through the open door and approached her she felt her heart flutter at the scent of his familiar musk. She beat back the urge to fall into his arms.

"Jules. What the hell are you doing here? You have to go, now." The firmness in his voice and the lack of an attempt to touch her pushed her over the edge. If there was going to be any kind of last-ditch explanation this is where he would make it, but there was nothing. Things were exactly as they seemed.

"You're a bastard," Jules hissed as she narrowed her eyes at him. "How could you do this to us?"

"Is Frankie here? Is she in Ohio?" His voice was low but panicked, clearly trying not to draw the eyes of everyone in the room.

"I'm sorry if the presence of your daughter in this state intrudes upon the second life you're living out here. Don't even say her name. You don't deserve her. You don't deserve either of us. We'll be gone by morning and don't bother coming back to Edenville. You aren't welcome."

"Jules, don't overreact—let me fix this. I can explain everything but I need you to leave now. I'll call you, and we'll work this out."

"We're done." Jules spun away as Lindsey came to her side, and they both strode at bullet speed toward the door. Though her words didn't say it, Jules hoped at any second, just before she reached their town car, Michael would stop her. Even if she hated him right now, even if there was no amount of explaining to fix this, she still wanted to know he was chasing her. But as she sank into the seat of the car and stared back at the marble steps, all hope was dashed. He had let her go, and now she'd have to find a way for her heart to let him go as well.

Chapter Eight

Jules let the hotel room door slam shut before she remembered Frankie would be sleeping by now. Piper's head popped out from around the corner and all Jules could manage was a pathetic wave before crumpling into tears.

"What happened?" Piper begged as she hesitantly moved toward Jules. "Did you see him? What did he say?"

"He told me to leave," Jules sobbed, toppling over her emotional dam and letting herself sink into the agony she was feeling. She hadn't wanted to fall apart in the car with Lindsey but now, here with her best friend, she knew she could give in.

"What do you mean he told you to leave? Tell me exactly what happened. There has to be some kind of explanation."

Though misdirected, Jules felt a burning anger that needed to be fired from her, and Piper was the closest target. "Could you, for one second," Jules barked, "stop being his friend and start being mine? There is *no* explanation. There is no excuse. He was there with his girlfriend. I saw her on his arm. The man at the door said they've known each other since high school. When Michael came up to me, all he told me was to go. That I couldn't be there. I think that's all pretty clear."

"I'm sorry, you're right. There is no excuse. I shouldn't have said that. You've always had my back, even with stuff with Bobby, and I'll do the same for you. Just tell me what you want to do now." Piper's voice was hushed and it reminded Jules of her sleeping baby just around the corner. That was all she wanted to do now.

Scoop her baby up and run back to Edenville, on foot if that's what it came to.

"I want to go home. I got the answer I came for, and I want to go back to Edenville and try to put all the pieces of my life back together. Who in the world would have thought I'd be twenty-seven years old and already have burned through two marriages?" She thudded against the wall as she pulled the pins out of her hair, letting it fall. She rubbed the ache out of her scalp, and she wished it would be that easy to comfort her heart.

"We can call the airline in the morning and get on the next flight home if that's what you want to do." Piper leaned against the wall and patted Jules's shoulder. Knowing Piper the way Jules did made the act even more impactful. Piper wasn't one to show much physical affection to anyone besides Bobby. She had worked so hard on her empathy and her ability to connect with people, but she'd never be deemed a hugger the way Jules and Betty were. The small gesture was her way of trying.

The light knock on the door sent both of them jumping, and Jules covered her thumping heart with her hand. "That scared me half to death. It's probably Lindsey checking on me. I said some pretty harsh stuff on the way here. I bet she's afraid I'll go back over there tonight." Without checking who it was, Jules swung the door open while patting her wet eyes with her free hand.

Standing with all the regal elegance of a 1930's Hollywood starlet was Michael's mother. Jules recognized her at once from the pictures Piper had pulled up online. Her mouth dropped open and words escaped her. It took all her willpower not to let the door slam right in the woman's face, simply out of sheer shock.

"I'm sorry to bother you tonight, dear, but I believe you were at my husband's memorial charity benefit tonight. My name is—"

Jules cut in with a wave of her hand as she regained her voice. "I know who you are. What are you doing here?"

"I saw you with my son and I need to know who you are. Judging by his reaction, you are clearly very important to him and I need your help."

"I'm sorry to disappoint you but I'm clearly not important to him, considering he asked me to leave the benefit. I can't help you with anything." Jules let the door begin to slide shut, but the woman's leg popped out from the slit of her dress and held the door open with her designer-clad foot.

"Please, I just want to know who you are. Are you his friend, or his girlfriend?" The woman's dark eyes drooped with a desperation that screamed for relief.

It wasn't Jules's job to maintain any of Michael's lies. Whatever web he weaved she wouldn't be a part of that. With that in mind she blurted out the truth. "I'm his wife."

"What?" the woman cried as though an arrow had just pierced her heart. She clutched at the doorframe trying to steady her now shaking legs. "When did he get married? How could he not tell me that?"

Jules's fears were confirmed. Not only did she know nothing about Michael's life in Ohio, the people here knew nothing about her. "He seems to be full of secrets. It came as quite a shock to me that my husband had a girlfriend at your event tonight. But now I know where I stand."

"A girlfriend? Michael wasn't at the event with anyone tonight. Who told you he had a girlfriend?" A seriousness fell over the woman's face, and she looked ready to fight, not with Jules per se, but with anyone who disagreed with what she knew to be the truth.

"When I walked in a man named Spencer told me Michael and his high school sweetheart, Elizabeth, had just left the dance floor. He said they were taking photos." Jules didn't want to let the small glimmer of hope that there was a misunderstanding penetrate her anger.

"Elizabeth and Michael haven't seen each other in probably seven or eight years. She is certainly not his girlfriend. The only reason they danced was at her adamant insistence. They're a terrible pair together, and I never really cared for her. Michael has no interest in her at all, and he's been avoiding her since the moment he came back into town."

"But Spencer," Jules shot back, ready to defend what she'd heard.

"Spencer is a rumor-spreading gossip who likes to feel important. You can't believe a word the man says, and everyone knows that about him. Michael and Elizabeth are strangers to each other at this point. I promise you that. But you, you are his wife, and you're a stranger to me." She shook her head and covered her heart with her hands as she took a few steps into the hotel room. Jules stepped aside to let her in, though she didn't really want to. She certainly hadn't invited her, but this woman didn't look like she was often denied entry anywhere in her life.

"I'm sorry you're finding out this way, Mrs. Cooper," Jules apologized, genuinely sorry Michael's mother had been left in the dark.

"Please, dear, I'm your mother-in-law. For goodness sake, call me Tabitha. It sounds like you have nothing to apologize for. It's my son who has that responsibility. He's in an awful way right now, and I'm desperate to get through to him, but I can't do it alone."

"He doesn't want me here," Jules retorted, stressing every word to make sure it was unavoidably clear.

"I'm sure that's not the case. He is lost right now. He and his father had a very complicated and tumultuous relationship. With his unexpected death, Michael never had the chance to make amends or get answers he so desperately wanted from his father. I think he's drowning in regret and grief right now even if he won't admit it. I'm sure he was just trying to shield you from that."

"You don't shield your wife from your feelings. You rely on her to help you through them. He's never told me a single thing about any of you. I never knew your name until I looked you up online. I ignored every red flag and now I'm paying the price for that. I'm sorry Michael might be hurting and misled you about his life, but I can't help you. I need to focus on getting my own life back on track." Jules wanted Tabitha gone, if that meant she evaporated into thin air or fell out the window, she didn't care. She was finding no comfort knowing she wasn't the only one being lied to by Michael.

Jules made her way toward the door, and as she reached for the handle, ready to gesture for Tabitha to leave, she heard the familiar late night cry of her daughter. The wails cut through the room and sent Jules's heart into her throat.

"Is that a baby?" Tabitha asked, stepping farther into the hotel room rather than taking the clear hint Jules was giving her.

"Yes," Jules said, giving up on Tabitha leaving and pushed past her to get to Frankie.

"I'll get her," Piper, who'd been noticeably silent but clearly observant, insisted.

"Is it your baby?" Tabitha whispered as though her voice were as weak as her shaky legs. "Is it Michael's baby?"

"Yes," Jules said flatly, trying to ignore the tears that formed in Tabitha's eyes and then spilled past her mascara to her cheeks. "She's our daughter."

Overwhelmed, Tabitha gave in to her tears, and Jules's empathetic heart could not let the woman fall to pieces without offering some kindness.

"Sit," Jules insisted as she pulled out the desk chair from the corner of the hotel room and wheeled it closer to the hallway where she leaned against the wall. "I'm sorry you found out like this. I'm sure this is upsetting." Jules wasn't convinced that her standing in this world, her practical peasant status, wasn't what was causing the tears.

"I'm not upset," Tabitha choked out as she blotted her eyes. "I just lost my husband and I had this overwhelming feeling my family was shrinking and it was suffocating to me, and now . . ." She let out a few more sobs before drawing in a deep breath. It reminded Jules of the old movie starlets of the black and white screen whose deep tears could strike you right through the heart. Whether she was acting or not wasn't clear, but the impact was the same. "Now all of the sudden I find out my family has grown. I'm a grandmother. You can't imagine how healing that is. How whole I feel again."

"I truly am sorry for the loss of your husband. I can't imagine what you must be feeling, and I'm glad finding out about us brings you some comfort." Jules didn't know what it was like to bury a husband, but she'd been grappling with losing Michael ever since he'd come out here. Now where did they stand? He didn't have a girlfriend, which was a positive. But he'd still hidden Jules and Frankie away like some dirty little secret he was ashamed of. He'd still insisted she leave his father's celebration of life tonight. Something still wasn't adding up, but a small glimmer of hope was wearing her defenses down.

"May I see her? I know it's late, but may I hold her? She's my granddaughter and I've never even met her. Please." Tabitha's eyes were wide and anxious, wet eyelashes fluttering in a panic.

How could Jules deny a woman something like this? If it were Betty wouldn't she want someone to give her that small gift, even if the situation was a mess?

"Of course you can." Jules slipped around the corner to the second room in the hotel to retrieve her daughter. Piper stood with her, doing the rhythmic, lightly bouncing dance that always calmed Frankie at night.

"She wants to meet Frankie," Jules said, reaching her arm out to take her daughter.

Piper's hushed voice was so low Jules had to strain to hear her. "I don't know if that's such a good idea. What do we really know about her? How did she find you so quickly and what does she want from you?"

"Could you stop playing skeptical detective for five minutes of your life? She saw Michael and me argue at

50

the party. She knows Michael is struggling and she's worried about him. She doesn't want to lose him. I'm sure she called the car service and used that information to find me." Jules stepped in and took Frankie from Piper's arms.

"Fine," Piper sighed as she folded her empty arms across her chest. Jules knew she hadn't won the debate, just staved off Piper's negativity about new people in their lives.

Tabitha's arms were already open and waiting as Jules rounded the corner with Frankie. She couldn't block the nagging feeling that handing her baby to a stranger, even if she was family, was wrong. But the warmth in Tabitha's eyes seemed so genuine and reminded Jules so much of how Betty looked at Frankie.

"Oh my goodness," Tabitha whispered as a nearly sleeping Frankie curled affectionately into her arms. "She looks like you, but I can see so much of Michael as a baby, too."

There was another reminder of Michael's disconnect from his past. Jules had never seen a single baby picture of her husband. She'd never known if Frankie and he had similar features at that age.

"I'll need to feed her before she goes back down," Jules apologized as she reached her arms out and lifted her daughter back into her arms. The expression on Tabitha's face was like swirled paint, all the colors recklessly swept together. Overwhelming joy brushed through sadness and pain.

"Please come to my house for lunch tomorrow," Tabitha begged as she shot to her feet, now seeming very steady. "I've just met you and your daughter; what is her name? I don't know your name either."

"My name is Jules, the baby is Frankie," Jules explained, peering down into her daughter's eyes, now at half-mast, ready to fall back into slumber if she were not fed soon. Jules knew that would mean she'd be up again in a few minutes crying to be fed.

"That's an adorable name. Please come to lunch tomorrow. I can't imagine you leaving now. Not after meeting you and knowing how kind you are. I don't want to lose Michael either. His relationship with his father always got between him and me, and if there is any silver lining to my husband's untimely death, I had hoped it would bring Michael and me closer."

"Tabitha, you seem like a very nice woman, and I'm sorry for your troubles with Michael, but I have my own. He abandoned us, lied, and then just tonight told me to leave. I'm sure you can tell from this not-so-fancy hotel we're staying in, I don't exactly come from your lifestyle. Knowing Michael isn't seeing another woman, I have to assume his not wanting me here has more to do with the drastic differences between my upbringing and your family."

"His father was an impossibly difficult man. If that is why Michael is keeping you away from us then it truly stems from his father, not from me. I've always just wanted Michael to be happy, with whomever that may be. But I do know his father had other plans for Michael and maybe that is why he is keeping you separate from us now. Please know I wouldn't care where you are from. You are family to me now and I beg you to consider coming to lunch tomorrow. It is my house and I want you there. And in my heart, judging by Michael's reaction after you left tonight, I am certain Michael wants you there too. He is just turned upside down right now."

"I guess we could come by for a little while. I'd like a chance for Frankie to meet her aunt as well." Jules looked down at her baby and struggled with the thought of facing Michael again.

"Josephine will be over the moon when she meets you both. She adores Michael and wants him to be happy. Please bring your friends as well. They are all welcome." Tabitha, seemingly rebounded from her emotional shock, made her way to the door.

"Thank you very much. We'll come for lunch then."

"A car will be here to pick you up at noon. One of my drivers will come and help you bring the baby and her things."

"I'd like to bring something. What will we be having? I could bring a dessert." Though Jules knew she wouldn't be whipping anything up in a hotel she thought it rude to show up empty-handed.

"What's your favorite food, dear? My chefs can make anything you like. No need to bring anything. Everything will be handled."

"I'm a down-home country girl at heart. I like any kind of southern cooking. I couldn't pick a favorite really."

"Don't you worry about a thing. You just get in the car when it comes to get you and the rest will work out." She leaned in and hugged Jules who entered the embrace stiffly, but then gave in. She needed a good hug tonight. "All of this will work out, and we'll be a big happy family."

Chapter Nine

Michael checked his phone again to see if Jules had replied to any of his text messages or calls. He had barely slept because the look on Jules's face had haunted him most of the night. Getting out of bed and facing the sun was making him feel sick to his stomach.

For the hundredth time the screen on his phone was still blank. Sending her away, begging her to leave the event, had ripped out his guts, but he didn't know of any other way. He wanted desperately to keep Jules from being pulled into this life he hated. The last thing he wanted was for her to be like a flimsy house in the wake of his mother's tornado: ripped up and destroyed. He was counting the minutes until he could get on a plane and get the hell out of here. Even though Jules had told him he wouldn't be welcomed back he had to believe he could explain and then, with time, she'd forgive him. He needed to believe that, or he'd go mad.

"Michael, you remember Isobel Corey from the Gazette?" Michael's mother hummed in her fake singsong voice as she approached him in the entryway of her home with the familiar woman in tow.

"Vaguely," Michael retorted flatly as the woman stretched her hand out for him to shake. "I recall years ago you wrote a piece on me proposing to Elizabeth even though that never happen. It caused quite a few problems for me, especially with her parents."

"People want a juicy story, Mr. Cooper. I think you can understand that, being from such a prominent family." Her pink shimmery lips curled into a devilish smile. Isobel met all the stereotypes of a society reporter.

From her power business suit to her over-styled blond hair. She was not a person; she was a persona.

"Is that what brings you here this morning? Hunting a hot story? I have to warn you, I'm not some kid anymore. I know my way around a libel lawsuit these days." Michael pulled his phone from his pocket, and checked for a response from Jules, and when there was still nothing he busied himself with scrolling through email. He wouldn't give his mother or Isobel much of his attention if he didn't need to. His flight was in four hours, which was all he'd focus on.

"I *am* writing an article, but I'm sure you'll like this one. It paints you as the prodigal child returning to swoop in and take the helm after your father's unexpected death. It might also mention something about you being the most eligible bachelor in the city." Her smug smile had Michael clamping his jaw down so tight his teeth ground together audibly.

"Your accuracy is as astounding as usual," Michael hissed as he began to walk away, no longer caring about keeping up appearances. Let them call him a jerk. Let people start asking questions about the perfect Cooper family falling apart. Once people started digging into his father's illegal business practices and embezzling, the house of cards would fall anyway. Why should he bother trying to hold it up in the meantime?

Before he could reach the hallway the loud chimes of the doorbell rang. The doorman, Ben, a man he'd known since he was five years old, scurried obediently past him toward the door. It was enough to slow Michael down, though he had no intention of stopping. It wasn't until he heard his mother's greeting that he froze in his tracks.

"Jules, you're here," she squealed, and Michael thought for sure he'd heard her wrong. It couldn't possibly be his wife here in his parents' home. His mother couldn't possibly know her name or have invited her here. But he knew full well, with his mother, anything was possible. When he spun around he saw Jules's fire red hair glimmering in the sunlight that streamed in behind her from the open door. Then in stepped Piper, holding Frankie in her arms. This was his worst nightmare come to life. With all his might he'd tried to keep these worlds from colliding, and now he could see he'd failed. His attempts had been no match for his mother's reckless selfishness.

"Hello Tabitha," Jules replied, and it nearly took Michael's feet out from under him to know his wife was on a first name basis with his mother.

"And who's this?" Isobel asked, her journalistic inquisitiveness taking over and ignoring any regard for privacy.

"This is my daughter-in-law, Michael's wife, Jules. And this," Tabitha cooed as she scooped Frankie into her arms, "is my granddaughter, François. Isn't she gorgeous?"

At that sight, the ringing in Michael's ears stopped and his seething anger took over. He marched toward his mother and plucked his daughter away. It had been hard to send Jules away last night, damn near impossible. But staring at the plump cheeks of his daughter and her red ringlets of hair, he knew he'd be sending no one away this morning. The smile that spread across the baby's face at the sight of her father was undeniably sweet. Though everything felt like it was crashing down around him, there was shelter beneath his daughter's little laughter.

56

"How in the world did you keep this quiet?" Isobel asked, punching something into her phone as she spoke. "You've fallen off the radar here and reemerge with a wife and daughter. People are going to go mad for this story. You'll be on the cover of the paper tomorrow. I can get a photographer here in an hour." Like a shark who'd gotten a whiff of blood across the ocean, the reporter was racing toward her prey.

"No," Michael boomed. "We're not posing for photographers and becoming tomorrow's gossip. We're eating lunch and leaving. My family isn't staying in Ohio."

"Do I sense some bad blood?" Isobel asked, with a raised eyebrow as her fingers froze on the keypad of her phone.

"Not at all," Tabitha cut in and put her arm around Jules. "You know how private Michael is about his personal life. He doesn't want his beautiful wife's face splashed across every paper tomorrow morning."

"Even without photos the story is going to run. I'd be mad not to be the one to break it. It's the media age, Michael." Isobel's apology was nothing but empty words as she tossed her phone back in her bag. "Sorry I can't stay for lunch now, Tabitha, but I have work to do. I'll show myself out." Not seeming to mind looking ridiculous or rude, Isobel broke into a near sprint as she headed out the door.

"Perfect, Mother. I'm sure that timing was no coincidence. Nothing you do ever is," Michael growled and then stopped suddenly as his daughter yanked on his ear and giggled again. It was damn hard being angry when he was holding the best thing that had ever happened to him.

"Jules," Michael started as he realized there was so much he wanted to say, but none of it was something he'd like to share in front of his mother. Now as his sister came running down the steps, skipping two at a time, he knew the conversation would need to wait.

"Are they here? Is this my niece?" Josephine shrieked as she nearly bowled Michael over to get to the baby.

"Yes dear, this is your niece and your sister-in-law, Jules," Tabitha explained, tightening her grip on Jules's shoulder. Jules was smiling broadly, clearly unaware of the danger these people carried with them. Michael glanced over his shoulder at Piper whose expression was flat as she took in every word passing between them.

That was what had made Michael and Piper great friends in the first place. A healthy skepticism and an ability to read between the lines of a conversation was something they both did well. Jules, on the other hand, gave everyone the benefit of the doubt.

"I can't believe you got married and had a baby and didn't tell us. Who does that?" Josephine asked as she scooped Frankie out of Michael's arms and began planting kisses on her chubby cheeks.

"It doesn't matter, we're all together now and that's what counts. Everything else can be worked out. Now lunch is about to be served," Tabitha announced through her plastered-on smile.

"I need to talk to Jules," Michael insisted.

"There will be plenty of time after lunch for that. I don't want the food to be cold." Tabitha began walking with her arm around Jules, ignoring Michael's words.

"Mother, I don't care about the damn food. I need to speak to my wife in private." Michael's booming voice

58

was not something Jules had heard frequently. He knew that, and judging by the look on her face, she didn't like it.

"Michael, we can talk right after lunch. Don't be so rude." Jules tilted her head and raked over him with her eyes as though he were suddenly a stranger.

"That's right," Tabitha smiled, turning and hugging Jules tightly. They all headed toward the large dining area, and Michael hung back for a moment to catch Piper's ear.

"This is bad," he said in a grumbling whisper. "She doesn't understand what's going on here."

"That's because you left without telling her. You didn't tell any of us," Piper whispered back, her face washed with worry.

"We're leaving after lunch. All of us are getting on a plane and getting the hell out of here. I need you to help make sure that happens."

"Fine. But why?" Piper asked, staring up at Michael.

"Because you trust me."

Chapter Ten

Seeing Michael holding Frankie had settled the rough seas of Jules's heart for a moment, but the tide turned again when she heard him bark madly at his mother. Since she'd met him, Michael had been a constant beacon of self-control. He maneuvered situations with the utmost respect for people. Yet he was treating his own mother like garbage. Tabitha was right, something was very wrong with him.

All thoughts of Michael evaporated for a moment as the two large doors to the dining room were opened by white-gloved men in tailored suits. The room was massive and embellished with gold trim and scrawling floral patterns across the walls. The length of the table was greater than Betty's entire kitchen and dining room combined. With dark mahogany furniture and tall, elegant centerpieces, the room looked fit for royalty.

Jules had daydreamed many days away, thinking about eating in a room like this. She was one of those small town girls with big city tastes. When other girls were playing with dolls, she was cutting out clothes from fashion magazines and mixing and matching designs. Rather than being boy crazy, for years Jules was clothes crazy. She drooled over fashion and as she got older that morphed into interior design as well. Though she could never afford it, that never stopped her from imagining it as a part of her life.

"In honor of Jules I had Genevieve prepare some southern dishes I'm sure you'll love. Perhaps even as much as your mother's." Tabitha gestured to each chair letting everyone know his or her place. "You'll be here by me, Jules, and Michael you'll be across over there."

Jules watched as Michael ground his teeth together and rolled his eyes. She couldn't believe how different and disrespectful he was being and she was actually glad not to be sitting next to him.

"You can put the baby right here." Tabitha smiled widely as she gestured toward a cream-colored highchair.

"That's a Bebe-Alesio highchair, isn't it? They're imported from Italy. I heard they only made a hundred of them," Jules swooned, running her hand along the fabric seat as though she were touching a treasure.

"It is," Tabitha said with a breathy laugh. "You really know your designers. I can tell you have wonderful taste."

"I'm a little bit of a fashion addict." Jules felt her cheeks flush as she slid Frankie into the beautiful plush seat.

"Have you spent much time in Paris? The dresses there are head and shoulders above anything you can find in the States." Josephine took a seat next to Michael, and Piper sat on the other side of Tabitha. Jules felt a lump grow in her throat as she tried to answer Josephine's question.

"I haven't been to Paris. I'd love to go someday." Jules took the napkin that was elegantly folded into some kind of bird and opened it as she placed it across her lap. She knew her cheeks were now burning fire engine red.

"We'll have to all see Paris this summer. It's a wonderful place for Frankie to visit, and you and I can meet with some designers for some special tailor-made dresses." Tabitha patted Jules's leg and then waved for the men in the corner of the room to start serving.

"I wouldn't have anywhere to wear designer dresses," Jules said, clearing her throat. "Back in

61

Edenville we don't have many galas. Since I've had Frankie I'm lucky to get out of yoga pants on an average day. I love beautiful fashion, but I don't wear it. Admiring it in magazines is about as close as I get."

"I know exactly what you mean," Tabitha comforted as she turned to face Jules.

"Really?" Michael asked with an arrogant tone. "How exactly can you relate to that? You never wear the same dress twice."

Jules shot daggers from her eyes at her rude husband. She felt like picking up her fork and launching it at him.

"I'm not just talking about fashion. Becoming a mother for the first time is life-altering. In those first months after I had you I spent plenty of days in sweat pants and just feeling . . ." Tabitha put her hand over her heart as she seemed to contemplate the right word. "I don't even know what to call it. Overwhelmed I guess. I've done a lot of things in my life but the most difficult experience was the first year of Michael's life."

Jules felt warmth spread across her chest just hearing someone else voicing the way she'd been feeling. It was hard. She was overwhelmed. "Exactly," she sighed, wiping away a stray tear before it could fall.

"I didn't know you were feeling that way," Michael cut in, looking genuinely concerned, the smugness falling from his face.

"Forget it," Jules sniffed. "I'm just glad to be here so Frankie and I can meet more family."

"It takes a village," Tabitha said as she leaned back and gestured for the man serving the peas to take them away. Something must have been wrong with them based on the way she turned up her nose, and the man reacted quickly to get them replaced.

"My mother, Betty, says that often." Jules couldn't for the life of her figure out what had driven Michael to hide her away from these people. They seemed delightful and perfectly comfortable that she wasn't from as prestigious of a family as they were. But all she could read was he seemed incredibly angry with his mother.

"I hope to meet her someday soon. From what you've told me she seems absolutely lovely." Tabitha glanced down at the new bowl of peas being presented to her and gave a nod that they were acceptable.

Piper's voice came out in a stronger tone than Jules imagined she meant it to. "She's an amazing woman as long as she likes you. If you cross her or her family she's as fierce as anything I've ever seen. A force to be reckoned with."

"Piper," Jules shot back, leaning forward and giving Piper a look as though rudeness might be contagious around this table.

"Then she and I will have an abundance of things in common." Tabitha's cool face was level as she replied.

"Actually I couldn't think of two people more different in this world than you and Betty," Michael scoffed, and he was met with the sharp slamming of a fork by his sister against the fine china plate in front of her.

"You really just can't help yourself, can you? You have to come back here after all these years and still cause problems. I understand you and Dad couldn't see eye-to-eye, but Mother and I have done nothing wrong. You are the one who ran away and hid your new family from us. We deserve more than that. Mom deserves your respect."

63

Michael's mouth opened and then abruptly closed. Jules felt a wave of relief when he didn't escalate this argument any further. After his chest rose and fell with a few centering breaths, he stared down at his plate and spoke. "We're leaving after this lunch so there won't be any need to worry about my attitude after that."

Josephine rolled her eyes and pushed her chair back from the table. "Then let me move things along for you and end this meal now."

"Josephine," Tabitha said in a steely tone, "sit down. We aren't going to solve anything like this. Every family has its hardships. This has been a difficult week for all of us, but let it be a starting point for some healing."

Michael's audible huff grated on Jules who was starting to feel terrible for Tabitha. She never imagined her husband would be a petulant child whose attitude matched that of any pubescent with a chip on his shoulder. Tabitha was clearly trying, and she'd gone so far as to chase Jules down last night.

"I am very sorry for the loss of your father, Josephine. I lost my dad twelve years ago and it's not easy. Even to this day I struggle with not having him around. That's why it's so important to hold on to the family you do have. My mother says family is like a song, some notes are in tune, some are out, but the music is always beautiful because it's yours."

"That's so lovely, Jules." Tabitha sniffled a bit as she drew in a deep breath and placed her napkin down on the table. Hardly anyone had eaten, but appetites seemed to have evaporated under the hot glow of tension around the table. "I know you want to leave, Michael, but please let me show you one thing before you go. It's important to me that you see it."

"Of course we will," Jules answered as she rested her hand Tabitha's shoulder and took note of the buttery soft silk of her bright blue kimono sleeve top. "I'll help you clear the table and then you can show us whatever you like."

"We don't clear the table," Josephine laughed, pushing her plate forward as though the idea of carrying it to the kitchen was ludicrous.

"They pay people to do that," Michael grumbled as he pushed his chair back and stood.

Tabitha was trying to ignore the awkwardness as she continued. "I know it's a bit over the top but when I got back here last night the idea of being a grandmother just swept me off my feet. I couldn't help myself." Tabitha lifted Frankie from the highchair and rested her maternally on her hip.

"Let me wipe her hands, Tabitha," Jules said, rushing toward Frankie with a napkin. "She'll get food on your shirt."

"Oh, I couldn't care less if she does. That's what babies do. I'll take precious little finger prints all over this house again in a heartbeat."

At that Jules felt her tense shoulders relax. These people weren't painfully pretentious when it came to her or Frankie. Their wealth was apparent, but it didn't make them terrible people.

"Come on with Grandmother," Tabitha sang as she waved them all to follow her out of the room. Jules had to admit it did feel a bit strange to hear the woman call herself Grandmother, but that was what she was. And equally odd was watching the staff swoop in and silently clear the table of the food and dishes. Jules stayed back for a moment looking at her plate wondering if she should just grab it and take it to the kitchen. "I can help you," she said with a soft smile as she reached for a few dishes and stacked them up. "I do mountains of dishes at home."

The smallest of the women clearing the table froze and became immediately uncomfortable at the sight of Jules helping out. Everyone else had stepped out of the room with Tabitha but the tiny woman still spoke in a whisper. "Please don't, ma'am. Mrs. Cooper will not be pleased with us if she sees you doing that. It's not proper for you to clear the table."

"That seems silly to me. I'm the one who made the mess. I could at least help clean it up. It's no trouble at all."

"No trouble to you, I'm sure, but it'll mean trouble for us," the man in the white gloves whispered anxiously as he took the pile of plates from Jules's hands. "Please, ma'am, we can appreciate your kindness, but we can't accept it." Scurrying to get the rest of the dishes off the table quickly and quietly, the staff went into overdrive. Jules stepped slowly out of the room as she heard the chatter of the staff fading away out the opposite door. A hushed man's voice was all she could make out. "I knew those peas wouldn't be good enough. I tried to warn the chef but she didn't listen. I guess this will be her last night here."

"Everything all right, dear?" Tabitha asked as Jules finally sidled up to them. She watched Michael quickly pluck Frankie out of his mother's arms, and she took note of the dark circles below his eyes and deep worry lines on his forehead. Something was eating at him. The last week had been the most confusing time of her life and she was plumb full of doubt and fear. But one thing was apparent:

her husband was hurting. Whether his reasons were justified or not wasn't clear, but for the first time since meeting Tabitha Jules felt the bell of tentativeness ring in her confused brain. Michael had a track record of being a painfully accurate judge of character and a man who doled out second chances to those who'd earned them. If he had dug his heels in deep here and was angry to the point where he didn't want to see his own mother holding his daughter, then maybe it was time for him to start talking and Jules to start listening.

Betty had told her just before she boarded the plane: *Every apple has its spots but if you don't eat around them you'll starve.* This week had been the bruise on their apple, and without Michael's love she did feel like she could starve. So maybe it was time to flip this thing over and take a bite out of the other side.

Chapter Eleven

Michael was preparing himself for anything. A surprise from his mother could genuinely be anything. There were no limits on what she would do to get her way.

"I went a little over the top and I'm going to apologize ahead of time. It's just that last night when I found out I had a granddaughter this pain in my heart was a little bit less." His mother swung open freshly painted white French doors to a room that used to be a second or third guest room.

"Oh my word," Jules gasped, and Michael felt a twinge in his chest at the glow that took over his wife's face. This room, this newly decorated nursery adorned with pink frills and pale green accents, was something Jules had likely dreamed of from the moment she found out she'd be a mother. This was his mother's power play and, judging by Jules's dropped jaw, it was making an impression.

"How did you do this, Mother?" Michael asked, a sharp pain darting through his temple.

"You know me, when I put my mind to something it gets done. I called in the big designing guns and they worked through the night. They were putting the finishing touches on it until about fifteen minutes ago. Through that door is a guest room so you can be close to Frankie at night. That should make things easy."

"We're leaving, Mother." Michael drew in a deep breath and locked eyes with Piper who looked like she had a rock in her stomach.

Blatantly ignoring his words, his mother continued, "Jules, I need to talk to Michael for a moment. Please

68

look around the room and let Frankie play with those toys in the corner. They are the absolute latest technology in educational toys. If you need to feed her, that rocking chair is the smoothest and most comfortable on the market. Please make yourself at home."

"Tabitha," Jules opened her arms wide and pulled her in for a tight hug. "This is so unbelievably kind of you. I can't believe you were able to do this so quickly." She took Frankie from Michael's arms and turned her back on him before he could even get his words of protest out. Jules and Frankie were already spread out on the plush carpet stacking up rings and digging through a pile of stuffed animals.

Piper was still looking like a statue in the corner of the sparklingly clean room as Michael reluctantly stepped outside with his mother.

"If you think you can buy her you're wrong. Jules values real things in this world not material things. That's something you wouldn't understand." Michael planted his feet on the marble floor and grounded himself, knowing nothing his mother could say right now could get him to stay. Nothing.

She shut the door and let the silence hang between them for a long moment. "Michael, I understand if you don't want to protect the image of this family. That might not be enough to keep you here, but protecting your sister should be."

"Jo has made it perfectly clear she is a grown woman and doesn't need anything from me. She's chosen the life she wants and it seems very similar to the one you have. If she has to bear witness to Dad's fall from grace, and yours as well, maybe that's just how it has to be." Michael wasn't truly so cold that he didn't care about his sister's feelings, but he had his wife and child to worry about first. They all belonged back in Edenville, not here in Ohio, while he did damage control that would likely fail anyway.

"It's not ruining her image of your father I'm worried about. She's in trouble. She needs your help, and I know you won't walk away and let her get hurt. You don't have it in you." Her face was stone serious as she dropped her voice to just above a whisper.

"What are you talking about?"

"You know firsthand what your father was capable of. The reason you left—well, he did the same thing to Josephine. She just doesn't know it yet."

"Stop talking in code, Mother. You have exactly sixty seconds to explain yourself or I'm taking my family and getting the hell out of here."

"As Josephine was finishing college your father convinced her that her best shot at a successful career was a hardy résumé. He began getting her invested in the company and charities. He gave her little jobs and she became immersed in the business. Your father began switching some responsibilities over to her, telling her how proud he was to have her on his team. What he was really doing was taking the most toxic assets and those impacted most by his illegal activities and moving them over to her. He was maneuvering himself free of any responsibility and putting it on her shoulders. His plan was after Wilson, her fiancé, was out of law school he'd move the rest as though it was a wedding present."

"How bad are we talking?" Michael could feel sweat beading on his forehead. He didn't even bother asking his mother if she were serious; she was correct that he did know what his father was capable of. He'd come so close himself to being buried under his father's crimes.

"Very bad. It's misappropriation of charity funds. Embezzling. Extortion and quite a few SEC violations. It's much worse than when he did it to you. If you don't step in, and do something she'll go to jail."

"What am I supposed to do? I'm a lawyer not a magician. I can't make things disappear."

"Your father's business associates want to see you at the helm in his place. Everyone is panicking that all the back room deals and lies are going to come crumbling down. It's simply a matter of time before someone exposes what they know in order to protect themselves. I need you to speak with them and work through some of it. Assure them. Then take every legal measure to push the responsibility back on your father and off your sister. She needs you, Michael."

There it was. That impossible-to-ignore lighter fluid that set his core ablaze. He was willing to watch his sister have to witness the wake of his father's crimes but he wasn't able to sit back and let her drown in it.

"Your wife and daughter are here now. They're happy and comfortable and you can stay and fix this now. A week or two and you could save Josephine. Isn't that worth it?"

"So that's what this was all about. Chasing Jules down and bringing her here was just a ploy to sweeten the pot to get me to stay."

"I'm sorry your father has put you in this position."

"Please don't act as though your hands are clean in all this. You are as guilty as he is. How could you let him do this to your daughter?"

"I didn't know until a couple days before he died. I thought it was different this time. I assumed he was working with Josephine for her own good, not his wicked intentions."

"Even if you didn't know he was betraying her you still spent the money he brought into this house. You knew how he got it, you knew it was earned on the backs of hard working people and stolen out from under them. It never stopped you. Every gala you've thrown, every designer dress you buy—it's all stained with his dirty money, and you let it continue. You stayed with him through every mistress and scandal he fought to keep quiet. You aided him in all of this. Jo doesn't deserve to be left holding the bag, but you do."

"Everything I did was to afford you the education and life that was built for you. Without it there would have been no expensive cars or private island vacations. You benefited greatly from that. You were happy. I never heard you complain."

"I didn't even know what happy was until I moved to Edenville and met my friends. I wasn't rich until I had a house full of people money couldn't buy. I feel sorry for you because you'll never understand that. But I can assure you that cycle ends with me. Frankie will not grow up in this environment. She will not be fooled into thinking servants and diamonds make you a better person. They don't."

"I applaud your convictions," his mother retorted sarcastically. "I'm sure you have a darling little life out there in the country. Are you so sure your wife doesn't want more? I saw her eyes light up at that highchair today."

"I won't bother trying to explain it to you, Mother. It's a gene you don't have, but there is such a thing as simple pleasures, and our life is full of them. I'll stay one week and whatever I can do in that timeframe I will. I'll do it for Jo, but after that my family and I go back home, and if you want any contact with us from there on, you can do it through me."

"Daniel Robertson is upstairs in your father's office waiting for you," Tabitha said with a victorious smile as she opened the doors to the nursery.

Michael's blood boiled at the idea that his mother had been so confident in the outcome of this conversation she'd already lined up Michael's first meeting.

"Let him wait. I'm talking to my wife first." He stepped back into the room and looked down at his daughter who was cramming the trunk of a rubber elephant into her mouth.

"It's a teething toy," Jules explained. "It's completely nontoxic and one of the best ones on the market. It's from France. I read about it in a parenting magazine."

"Nothing but the best for my granddaughter." Tabitha smiled as she pushed a bit of lint off her shirt. "Are you going to tell them the good news, Michael, or should I?"

"We'll be staying for a week," Michael said with a sigh, feeling like he'd just hammered a nail into his own coffin.

Josephine rounded the corner of the nursery and skipped into the room. "Did I hear that right? You're staying? That means you'll be here for my engagement party this weekend."

73

"Yes, we'll be there." Michael's heart ached as he looked his sister over now. He had started to perceive her as a miniature version of his mother, but in reality she was still just his baby sister. She'd grown up in this toxic environment and he couldn't blame her for taking on so many of her parents' traits. Deep down at her core he still recognized her.

"I can't wait to tell Wilson. He's going to be so excited. Thank you for staying. I know we've been arguing but it means so much to me to have you there. Especially with Dad gone now."

"I'm going to be doing a lot of stuff with Dad's affairs so you won't see much of me but I'll be at the party for sure."

"I'm going to call Wilson now." Josephine jumped up and threw her arms around Michael. "I knew you'd stay." She squealed with joy.

"There are still so many things to do for the engagement party so I'll be on my way too. I'm excited to have you here with us a little longer," his mother professed.

"Me too," Jules said, squeezing Frankie tighter in her arms and taking another look around the new nursery.

"I'll need your help getting everything ready for the party. It's a lot of work and with the funeral I've lost some time. I have a feeling you'll be a wonderful party planner."

"I'd love to help." Jules was like a kid on Christmas morning when faced with the idea of planning an extravagant party.

"And you too, Piper. All hands on deck as they say."

"I'm afraid I'm not much of party planner. I don't have any of those skills at all." Piper shrugged her shoulders and pursed her lips in a transparently non-apologetic smile.

"I'm sure you must be great at something." Tabitha waved her hand dismissively.

"I'm a great judge of character," Piper shot back, locking her eyes on Tabitha. "And I have a knack for finding things out."

Once again Jules narrowed her eyes at Piper as though she couldn't believe the blatant rudeness. Michael on the other hand drew in a deep breath to hold back a laugh.

"Well then, we'll put you at the table with Martha Wolver. I'm dying to know her secrets. Michael, don't forget your meeting. Daniel is waiting for you." Tabitha deflected the warning and headed out of the nursery as though she didn't have a care in the world.

"That was rude," Jules said in a hushed voice. "What the hell has gotten into both of you? Michael, it's like I don't even know you. I've never seen you treat anyone the way you're treating your own family."

"We need to talk," Michael said, shutting the door to the nursery.

"I thought your mother just said you had a meeting." Jules picked up Frankie and placed her in the bright white crib adorned with pink and green sheets.

"He can wait. You need to know what's going on here. I didn't decide to stay because I had a change of heart about my family. I haven't."

"I don't want to have this conversation in the five minutes you have before a meeting. I'm still very upset about how you left, about the lies and secrets, *and* how you're acting."

"My father put my sister in danger by bringing her in as a part of his business and charities. If I don't fix it, she could go to jail."

"Why would he do something like that?" Jules furrowed her brows and Michael felt sorry for her. She truly didn't realize what people were willing to do for power and money. It made her a target here.

"He was an arrogant, power-hungry bastard who didn't care about anyone but himself."

"Don't speak ill of the dead," Jules shot back, making a hasty sign of the cross.

"I need you to please consider going home, Jules. I know my mother can be very convincing, but she isn't the person you're seeing today. It would take me all day to explain to you how dangerous she is, but please, in lieu of that, can you please just trust me?"

"You've shaken my trust in you, Michael. I need you to take responsibility and understand that keeping your family a secret from me, and me from them, was wrong. I can see that something about this place is eating at you and I now believe maybe you made your choices because you thought you had to, but I deserve the opportunity to form my own opinions. Frankie deserves the chance to know her family. All of them. I want to stay for the party."

This was no surprise to Michael. He knew the answer before he asked the question. Jules would not leave now; she was too stubborn for that. "I won't be around much. If I want to make an impact and help my sister in only a week then I'll be busy the whole time. I want you to be wary of my mother, of the people she introduces you to. Please remind yourself over and over again she does nothing unless there is a benefit to her."

"Well maybe that benefit is being a grandmother. From the sound of it you haven't been back here in quite some time. People do change. We've seen it in our own lives. I want to give her a chance. I want you to give her a chance."

"I'm sorry, Jules, I'm all out of chances with her. The only reason I'm staying here is to protect Jo. My sister deserves better than the hand my father dealt her."

"I can't imagine what your mother would have done to make you feel this way. It's not like you at all." Jules pulled the sage green satin curtains closed, bringing near darkness to the room.

"I should have told you everything from the beginning. You deserve to know the truth and what we're dealing with here. That's my mistake. I'm truly sorry for that. I know I damaged what we have, but I will work hard to repair every single dent and scratch. I need you to remember who I was before all this happened. Please remember how I made decisions and what I did for our friends and family. I think you always believed in me. You believed everything I did was to protect people I love. Just hold on to that for me. I'm still that man. I'm still your husband and Frankie's father and you can trust me. You have to." Michael felt on the verge of losing control as he pleaded with his wife. His eyes danced with worry and desperation, and Jules came in to rescue him from it.

"I will," she assured him. "I know you are always trying to keep us all safe. I won't forget that. Let's just talk tonight. You can tell me everything. I want to know what you're going through. Maybe I can help." For the first time in nearly a week his wife's arms reached around his waist and pulled him in. With her fire red hair beneath his chin he breathed her in, squeezing her with the conviction of someone who thought might have lost his chance to ever do it again. "I've got to get Frankie down for her nap. And I have to say, this room makes me look forward to hours of rocking her. Now you go to your meeting and good luck."

Jules shooed Piper and Michael out of the nursery and closed the doors tightly.

"What exactly are we dealing with here, Michael?" Piper asked, her face painted with worry.

"I'm glad you're here, Piper. I knew you'd be able to see through my mother's bullshit. You're going to have to help me."

"You know I will, just tell me what you need."

"The best thing that could happen in my mother's eyes is for me to stay here for good. That would mean I could run all my father's mess long term and keep her income flowing without a hitch. She won't be satisfied with just his life insurance. She'll want more and more. Now she has a grip on the two things that mean to most to me in the world. She'll do anything to use that to her advantage. Jules and I are on shaky ground and my mother is a master at manipulation. It isn't enough for me to just tell Jules she can't be here, or my mother can't be trusted. She won't hear that. I'm going to be completely invested, dealing with my sister's problems so I can get us out of here quickly. Please keep an eye on her. You just keep being that skeptical, untrusting pain in the ass you always are, and keep Jules safe while she is the warm and blindly accepting person she is."

"I promise," Piper said, not an ounce of hesitation in her voice.

"I think there have been a million reasons why you and I are lucky to have Jules and Betty and Bobby in our lives. We need them. They soften our edges and make us more human. But in this situation, Jules needs us. She needs our cynical caution to keep her from getting sucked in here."

"She can be pretty stubborn. It's not going to be easy to get her to listen once she's headed in one direction."

"By any means necessary, Piper. Whatever you need to do, I'll support you. Just take care of her."

"By any means necessary," Piper parroted back, shaking her head in agreement. "This should be fun."

Chapter Twelve

Michael unbuttoned the sleeves of his shirt at the wrist and rolled them to his elbow before entering his father's office to face a man he'd looked upon like an uncle. Daniel Robertson was the investment broker who had helped his father build his fortune. Michael could only imagine how many onion-like layers their friendship had.

As he pushed open the heavy dark wood door he assumed he was about to find out.

"Michael, damn, you've changed so much." Daniel stood in the corner of the office eyeing old photographs hanging on the wall. Other than his hairline, which had receded by at least three inches, he seemed to have changed very little over the past eight years. He was a fit man, probably hitting the gym a few days a week to stave off the effects of age. That was something he and Michael's father argued about often. Daniel was always trying to encourage his dad to work out with him. After his father's first heart attack twelve years ago Michael thought he might start taking Daniel's advice, but Michael Cooper, Senior was too stubborn for that. He liked his cigars and his scotch as well as his steaks.

"Sorry to have kept you waiting," Michael lied as he reluctantly took a seat in his father's large leather chair. There was a time in his childhood when he'd put on a tie and pretend to be his father, even though his feet dangled off the large chair.

"Not at all, I'm glad you took this meeting with me. I know you must be up to your eyeballs sorting out your father's different partnerships and agreements. I'm just one spoke in that wheel." Daniel took a seat across from Michael and folded his hands in his lap.

"I've barely scratched the surface, really. But I have a plan in mind. It's just a matter of executing all the paperwork." Michael leaned back in his chair and took in the musky scent of his father's cologne and cursed the flood of memories that came with it.

"I'll be honest, Michael, that's good to hear. There is a lot of chatter out there. People are worried about what kind of approach you'll take with the business. You've been gone so long that you're a bit of a wild card." The look of relief on Daniel's face was short-lived.

"I'm closing it all down," Michael said flatly. "I'm scaling and legitimizing the manufacturing business. The charities, the back-room deals, and flat out stealing ends now. The only reason I'm leaving the manufacturing line of business open is because I don't want to put hardworking employees out on the street in this economy. I'm going to make it dummy proof and turn it over to someone I can trust—if I can find anyone out here who fits that bill."

"Michael," Daniel stuttered his name out as he furrowed his brows in disbelief. "You can't be serious. I don't think you understand what you'd be walking away from. You're talking about millions of dollars. I don't know what kind of life you're living down South, but it's not going to compare to what you'd have if you kept on the track your father has set up."

"My life back in Edenville is priceless to me, and I'm not going to get sucked into this world and turn into my father. You of all people know what he was capable of, how toxic his life was. I've already made my decision. There isn't anything you can say to change my mind.

Let's just talk about how we sever any agreements you and my father had."

Daniel hesitated as he loosened the collar of his shirt by releasing a button as though he were suffocating. "I was not expecting this. You know I know a lot about your father. I mean, I have a lot I could hold against him."

"And I'm guessing tonight when I open his safe and tomorrow his safety deposit boxes I'll find an equal amount of incriminating evidence against you. He's dead. If you expose him now the only person you'll hurt is Josephine. I have to imagine even you have a scrap of decency that will keep you from doing that. And if not, then the risk of being exposed yourself should do it."

"When you go through the paperwork you'll see I owed your father two hundred thousand dollars. He put some capital behind an investment of mine and it didn't pan out."

"Consider your debt paid. The only thing I want in return is your word that you'll destroy anything incriminating you have on my father."

"I'll make that deal. But I don't think it matters." Daniel gnawed anxiously at his lip as he seemed to choose his words carefully. "Your mother will never approve of your shutting everything down."

"My father left all decisions to me in his will. She got the life insurance, and as punishment I got this mess to clean up. My mother has no legal standing in any of this."

Daniel let out a low chuckle as he spoke. "I've never known your mother to need legal standing in anything to get her way. If you thought your father was a force to be reckoned with then you're misjudging your mother."

"I appreciate the warning." Michael nodded, hoping this would be the end of their conversation.

"It's not a warning, son, it's a guarantee. You'll be in for the fight of your life if you think you'll be able to pry this money out of your mother's hands."

"She has a hefty life insurance policy to sustain her. And I'll make sure the profits from the manufacturing business go to her."

"That business is barely profitable. It stays in the green because of those back-room deals you were talking about. She won't be able to maintain this lifestyle on that money for long."

"Then she can adjust her lifestyle to her means. The days of big charity banquets are gone. She can liquidate assets and live a damn good life."

"You've been gone too long, Michael. You forget what she's capable of when her way of life is challenged."

"I hope I can count on you to keep this quiet. If I have a fight ahead of me then at least I'll have the element of surprise."

"To be honest with you, since the day I went into business with your father I've been looking for a way out. How that man ever stomached the things we did I'll never know. I lost more nights of sleep than I can count and taxed my conscience to the brink of losing my mind some days. I'm glad you're cleaning all this up. You and your sister deserve better than to have to carry on this legacy." Daniel stood and showed himself to the door, waving for Michael to stay in his seat. "I know my way out. I just hope you know yours."

Chapter Thirteen

"I feel like a princess," Jules squealed quietly to Piper as she gestured for her to zip up the gown she'd just tried on. It was a deep emerald green that somehow perfectly matched her eyes. Embellished at the princess neckline with subtle crystals, it was the perfect mix of eye-catching elegance.

"It looks really nice on you," Piper said, looking completely uninterested in dress shopping from the second they'd stepped foot in the normally appointment-only designer boutique. Apparently Tabitha did not need an appointment.

"You hate this, don't you?" Jules asked, never taking her eyes off herself in the mirror. "This dress shopping is like your worst nightmare."

"I'm just worried about Frankie. She's been alone since you put her down for her nap." Piper shrugged.

"Come out, girls, I've got to see you in that dress," Tabitha called through the thick red velvet curtain separating them.

As they stepped out Tabitha and the associate behind the counter let out a gasp. "That dress was made for you," Tabitha said, gesturing for Jules to spin.

"Thank you so much. I feel so amazing in it." Jules ran her hands down the dress and took in how perfectly it fit her as she turned in a slow circle in front of the mirror.

"Then why the sad look?" Tabitha asked, stroking Jules's long red hair empathetically.

"Piper and I were just talking about Frankie being home while we're here. I'm wondering how she's doing,"

"First off, Nicolette has been a nanny and housekeeper in our home since Josephine was born. I

84

trusted her with my own child. But here," Tabitha assured, spinning her phone around for Jules to see it. "The whole house is wired with a security system. You can take a peek at her anytime you'd like. I remember what it's like that first year having a baby. You feel so exhausted and overwhelmed. You forget what it's like to look like this." Tabitha gestured to the full-length mirror on the wall for Jules to look at herself in the dress again. "Taking time for yourself makes you a better mother. Everyone needs to recharge and feel good every now and then. You wouldn't understand, Piper, because you don't have any children."

Jules felt the sting of that comment for Piper. She knew Tabitha was right, Piper really didn't understand how awful she felt lately, but it still wasn't the nicest way to make that point. "Thank you for showing me the security system. That makes me feel better." Jules smiled as she stared at herself in the dress again.

"After this Josephine is meeting us at the spa for a full workup. You're going to be so relaxed you might just melt." Tabitha clapped her hands excitedly.

"I thought you needed help planning the party this weekend. It's only four days away." Jules could hear the annoyance in Piper's voice and she hoped she wouldn't ruin the steps forward in her relationship with Tabitha.

"This is part of the planning. We'll all talk through more details while we get our hot stone massages. Have you ever had one, Piper?"

"I haven't," Piper replied flatly. "I'm not much for being touched by strangers. And I have some scars I don't like people seeing."

"Oh, that's terrible. You know I have a plastic surgeon I swear by. He could get rid of any kind of scar you have."

"Really?" Jules asked, her hand instinctually going to the place on her thigh where she bore the reminder of her run-in with the man who was hunting Piper.

"Yes dear, do you have some as well? I'm telling you he's a miracle worker. Let's get this dress boxed up, and I'll call him on the way to the spa."

"How much is the dress?" Jules asked, looking around for the price tag that didn't seem to exist. "I'll have to call Michael and just run it by him first."

"No, the dress is on me. Michael is working so hard to get everything back on track in his father's very messy business. The least I can do is buy you this dress."

The sales associate came over and handed Tabitha an electronic device for her to sign. "Did you want the fifty-six hundred dollars on your account, Mrs. Cooper, or should I just bill it to your platinum card here on file?"

"Let's use the platinum card," Tabitha chirped as she signed her name and smiled widely at Jules.

"Wait. This dress costs over five thousand dollars?" Jules squeaked, instantly going as still as a statue as though any sudden movement could cause the expensive dress to rip.

"It's from a French designer who only created three gowns with that fabric. You'll never see anyone else in that dress," the associate explained defensively.

"The dress is perfect. It's a very fair price for something that seems like it was made for you. It's my treat," Tabitha insisted.

"I can't wear a dress that costs that much. I'll never have anywhere to wear it again. It will be a waste."

"You can wear it to another event back home if you like," Tabitha said waving off her concern.

"We don't have events like this in Edenville. The closest thing is when the rodeo comes to town." Jules's cheeks burned hot red.

"Well then you'll just have to spend some more time here in the city to make good use of such an amazing dress," Tabitha offered as she shooed Jules back into the fitting room. Piper stepped in with her and helped her gingerly slide out of the dress now that she knew how much it cost.

"You can't seriously be thinking of letting her buy you this dress," Piper whispered as Jules slipped the gown back onto the hanger.

"She wants to do it. I don't want to insult her. Plus this engagement party this weekend is going to be very formal. I wouldn't have anything else to wear."

"What about the dress you wore to the gala?"

"I can't wear the same dress twice. There are people who will have been at the gala who will be attending the party. Plus that dress is practically peasant status. All I need is for someone to ask me who I'm wearing. I'd have to answer Ginny Lou Morrisville's special design that she makes in her basement on the weekends. That would be mortifying."

"Since when do you care what people think?"

"I don't, but this is a whole other world, Piper. The kind of place I've dreamed about being my entire life. You see me as this country bumpkin, but I know more about fashion and this lifestyle than anyone back in Edenville. You don't understand how I've been feeling lately. I need this right now. It's not about the dress it's about how I feel in it."

"Michael warned you to be careful. He obviously doesn't trust his mother. You aren't acting very cautious around her."

"He's grieving the loss of his father and trying to deal with being back here. I don't think it has anything to do with his mother at all. She's lovely. He needs to sort out how he feels. In the meantime I'm not going to treat his mother poorly if she isn't treating me that way."

Tabitha split the curtain open as Jules slipped her cotton shirt back over her head and interrupted their hushed voices. "We're all set. She's going to box the dress up and have it delivered to the house. We can head to the spa now if you Chatty Cathys are ready." There was a slight edge to her voice that implied she could hear what they'd been discussing and surely she wouldn't have liked the exchange. Jules's cheeks flushed as she prayed Tabitha hadn't heard Piper's opinion.

"I think I'll skip the spa." Piper stepped past them and was almost to the door before Jules slipped on her shoes. "I'm going to go check in with Lindsey at the hotel."

"Piper please consider staying with us at the house. We have plenty of room for you and Lindsey. Michael is working so hard. I'd like him to be surrounded by friends." Tabitha gave a wave to the associate as she headed toward the door with Piper.

"That sounds good," Piper agreed, and Jules sighed with relief that Piper wasn't letting her attitude get in the way of Tabitha's gracious offer.

As they all hit the sidewalk, Tabitha put her phone to her ear and gave an abrupt order to someone. "Piper, there will be a car here for you in just a few minutes. They'll take you back to your hotel and then over to the house for you to settle in. Jules and I will likely be late so the cook will fix you dinner."

Without waiting for Piper to respond, Tabitha and Jules were ducking into the waiting car and the driver was closing the door behind them.

"She means well," Jules explained as she fastened her seatbelt and slipped her lipstick from her purse. She'd gotten out of the habit of reapplying regularly and now she was forcing herself to make it a priority again.

"She seems sweet, just not accustomed to this type of lifestyle. I'm sure it's not how she grew up."

"If you only knew how she grew up you'd never look at her the same way. She's been through hell. As a matter of fact she was still going through it when we met her." Jules smacked her lips together smearing the red lipstick and tucked it and her mirror away again.

"Like what?" Tabitha asked, looking genuinely interested in what Jules had to say.

"It's kind of a long story, but she grew up in New York City. She was completely poor and badly abused. When she got older, the man she believed to be her father killed her mother and nearly killed her. That scar she mentioned was from him. He carved a number into her thigh. She was relocated to Edenville where I grew up. The problem was that man wasn't done with her. She and I became friends and in order to get to her, he kidnapped me. I have that same scar on my leg now. I hate it."

"You won't have to hate it for much longer. I'm going to get you in touch with my plastic surgeon. No one should have to be reminded of something so horrific. I can't believe you were kidnapped. What happened to the man?"

"He was killed. It was really crazy for a while. I didn't think Piper would survive it. And if she did I certainly didn't think she'd go on to live such a normal life. She married my best friend, Bobby, and she's going to school to help other children who are dealing with abuse. It's remarkable really."

"I'd say it is," Tabitha smiled. "It's remarkable you've remained friends with her. It sounds like she's brought quite a bit of chaos to your lives."

"She's brought a lot of good things too," Jules defended. "We're all very close now. My mother has taken everyone under her wing. Piper and Bobby are godparents to Frankie. We have a very good life in Edenville."

"I have no doubt you do. It's likely great for you and Michael, but have you thought about how it is for Frankie?"

"What do you mean?"

"Well, I just see you and think how much potential you have. You fit right in here. You're gorgeous, smart, and very sophisticated. You don't seem to be reaching your potential in Edenville. What opportunities are there really for someone like you?"

"None," Jules admitted, staring down at her chipping nail polish. It had been so long since she'd gone to the salon and had them done. She'd had to settle for painting them herself during Frankie's much too short naps.

"I'm sure Frankie could do well in a place like this. My children went to the best schools, saw the best doctors, and have benefited greatly from that. You know Josephine had a terrible speech delay. If not for the incredible intervention she received she'd never be as successful as she is today. Have you given thought to where Frankie will go to school?"

"She's just a baby," Jules shot back, missing her daughter immensely at the moment.

"Here she'd already be on a waiting list for kindergarten. The private schools are incredibly competitive. Now, because she is a Cooper, she'd have no problem getting in. There would be very little in this city she couldn't do with that last name. She could travel the world and so could you." Tabitha's face was lit with a kind of excitement that made Jules imagine what her life could be.

"Our home has been in Edenville. My mother is there. Piper and Bobby are there. I can't imagine leaving them," Jules explained. But the truth was she *could* imagine it. She had been since she tried on that dress a little while ago.

"It's a big city and we have plenty of property. It's not as though they couldn't spend time out here, too. You're thinking too much about logistics and how that works with your life today. You're thinking plane tickets and hotels. You need to be thinking private jets whenever you like and guesthouses. I'm not foolish. I understand that our life is a bit extravagant. But the benefit to that is limitless possibilities for accommodating anything."

"I suppose I never really thought about that. I guess if it meant we'd be able to spend time in both places or family could come to us whenever they wanted, I wouldn't mind being out here."

"I can't think of a thing in the world that would make me happier. We genuinely need Michael to run some of these business issues and the charities. We can't do it without him. But it doesn't mean he needs to be here all the time. You could spend summers here and winters down there. It's just something to think about. Michael isn't open to it right now, but I don't think he's really thinking about Frankie's future or even your happiness. You deserve to hop on a plane next week and spend the afternoon in Rome with Josephine and me while we pick out jewelry for the wedding. Frankie should be going to the best pediatrician with state of the art technology. I think deep down Michael knows that, but he likely doesn't want to take you from your home."

"Like you said, though," Jules cut in, "it's not as though home is that far away. Or that people couldn't come spend time with us whenever they wanted. It wouldn't be impossible to make it work. It's certainly something to think about."

"I'm so glad you feel that way. Now that I'm here with you I can't imagine not having you, Frankie, and Michael in our lives on a more regular basis. Now the only thing we have to do is figure out how to convince Michael that letting Josephine and me back into his heart is the right thing to do. I know he's never forgiven me for supporting my husband, but his father and I were married for thirty-four years. We were best friends. Having to choose between them was an impossible task, and I knew that Michael would land on his feet no matter what he did. His father needed me more," Tabitha croaked as a stray tear trailed down her face. She reached in her bag and grabbed a lace-trimmed handkerchief to dab at the wetness.

Jules reached her hand out and clutched Tabitha's shaking shoulder. "I completely understand. I can't imagine what it would be like to be in that position. Michael will come around. I believe that."

As the car slowed to a stop at a glass front building, Jules let her mind spin through all the ways she could help mend this broken family. Wasn't that what this group had done all along? Hadn't so many hearts been reunited through their efforts over the years? Surely Michael's family could be just one more wounded little birdy that they all nursed back to health.

The door to the car was pulled open, and like a switch being flipped off, Tabitha managed to regain her bubbly composure as she clasped the hand of a man helping her out of the car. And just like that, the whirlwind of pampering began. Before Jules could blink there was a sparkling water in her hand and the earthy smells of an upscale spa took over her senses.

"Get ready, dear," Tabitha squealed as she looped her arm around Jules. "You're about to have a life-changing experience."

Jules clutched the plush robe that had just been handed to her and she chanted silently: *I deserve this. I've earned this.*

Chapter Fourteen

Michael pushed another stack of paperwork to the side of his father's desk. He was making progress. Slowly but surely he was filing forms and understanding the depth of the problems his father had created. It was ugly, but as the clock above the door chimed eight thirty at night, he knew he had to take a break. He'd promised to talk to Jules tonight and explain more about his reasoning for keeping her from this place and why they needed to leave as soon as they could. She deserved that from him. And he hadn't held Frankie since just after lunch; the smell of her powdery skin was still lingered on the collar of his shirt.

As he pushed the large chair away from his desk he heard the familiar coo of his daughter's voice echoing up the hallway. Perfect timing. He got to his feet and headed for the door. Expecting to see his wife he peeked his head out playfully, ready to kiss her. Instead he was met with Piper's extended hand shoving his face away.

"What are you doing?" she croaked as she pushed his face back a little and adjusted Frankie on her hip.

"I thought you were Jules," Michael muttered, rubbing his cheek and extending his arms to take Frankie. His heart flooded with much missed happiness as she nearly leaped into his arms.

"Jules is still out with your mom. I thought she'd be home from the spa by now, but I guess they must have gone somewhere after." Piper wrung her hands nervously as she spoke.

"You were supposed to stay with her. I told you how conniving my mother is. You can't let her get her claws in Jules."

"I didn't want Frankie to be put to bed by some stranger. I knew you were busy trying to get the hell out of here. Plus I'm not sure there is all that much I can do to keep Jules from falling for your mother's attempts to impress her. Once she bought her a five thousand dollar dress this morning for your sister's engagement party everything I was saying fell on deaf ears. Jules is not pretentious or anything, but she's damn tired and you put her through the wringer coming out here. It's not taking very much to get her all caught up. You know as well as I do that Edenville has always felt too small for her. She loves this stuff, and she's finally getting a taste of it."

"So, what, you're giving up?" Michael asked, starting his tone rough and then softening the edges as he thought of his daughter in his arms.

"No, I'm letting you know that it's not going to be as simple as just telling Jules that your mom has an agenda or that she's selfish. You're going to need to really explain to her what's going on here."

"I was going to tonight but I guess my mother is keeping her out late to try to keep me from doing that. But come tomorrow morning everything will be different." Michael squeezed his daughter a little tighter as she rested her tired head on his shoulder.

"And what exactly happens tomorrow?" Piper asked, looking skeptically up at Michael.

"I'm going to take a play from my mother's book and see how she likes it. She won't know what hit her. Then she'll realize trying to get to me through Jules won't work."

"Your mother doesn't strike me as someone to back down just because her first plan doesn't work. She wants you here. She wants you running all this so she doesn't lose what she has, am I right?"

"Yes, but I have no intention of staying here and paying for my father's crimes. I won't turn into him. I won't watch my wife get sucked into the wake of my mother's insanity and selfishness. I'm ending this now. All of it."

"It sounds like you're starting a war."

"I'd fight a war to keep them safe. I know this is a different kind of danger than you've had in your life, and maybe it doesn't seem as bad, but it's just a different kind of bad; trust me. My mother will stop at nothing to keep this life going, but what she doesn't understand is there is no way to maintain the charade anymore. They got too greedy and it was all falling apart long before my father died. His death was just the tipping point. This was a long time coming."

"Is that why you left? You knew it wasn't sustainable?" Piper patted Frankie's back gently and Michael watched as the baby's eyes fluttered heavily, weighed down by the sandman.

"I left because my father betrayed me, and I couldn't look at him the same way again. I idolized him, and he ripped my heart out and stomped on it." The heaviness of this topic wasn't Michael's style. He was the one who broke tension through jokes and levity. Luckily he and Piper were a lot a like.

"Geesh, the guy I thought was my father only tried to stab me a couple times. He never tried to rip my heart out," she joked.

"The only thing we can do," Michael whispered, watching his daughters eyes finally close as she fought to stay awake, "is do a better job than they did. This baby is never going to go through any of that. She belongs in Edenville. We all do. We're better there. Now I need you to keep doing your best to keep Jules focused. Things are going to blow up tomorrow. I need her to come out on my side."

"I'm sure she will. Your mom might be good, but not that good. Jules loves you and she's not going to take your mother's side just because she spent one day at the spa."

"Don't underestimate her or the spa. That place messes with your head."

"I never pegged you for a pedicure kind of guy," Piper joked quietly as Michael handed her back a sleeping Frankie.

"I'm embarrassed how well I know my way around a spa. I think I missed the deep sea mask the most when I left for Edenville."

"You are so lucky Bobby isn't here to listen to this. You'd never live it down."

"Joke all you want. When we're all old I'll be the only one without wrinkles. Then who will be laughing?"

"We'd still laugh at you." Piper turned toward the door and patted Frankie's back rhythmically.

"I can put her to bed," Michael offered, feeling like he was asking too much of his friend. All of this seemed like too much to expect from someone. "I feel bad leaving you to yourself in this big boring house."

"Lindsey is here. Your mother invited her to stay in one of the spare bedrooms. There seems to be no shortage of those. I hope you don't mind but I filled her in on what's going on. Now she's got her police antennas up and she's treating everything like she's working a case here."

"Good, tell her to keep it up. I don't know what my mother will do come tomorrow. It can't hurt to have a cop around. Does my mother know what she does for a living?"

"No, they haven't formally met yet. I don't think Lindsey intends to tell her though. I think she's been out of work too long while her leg heals, and she thinks she's undercover here."

"Let's keep it that way. She can be our secret weapon if we need her."

"You really think it's going to come to all that?" Piper asked as she adjusted a snoring Frankie slightly.

"I'm not taking any chances. You just keep Jules focused on what's important if you can. Keep reminding her how much our life means to us back in Edenville and how she has always trusted me. I don't know if I'll ever be able to thank you for being here and doing this for me."

"Oh yes, you'll be in my debt, as long as you don't count every single situation you've bailed me out of since we met. If you weren't saving me from my past you were saving me from myself. I'll do my best to think of ways to keep Jules from getting swept up in this."

"I don't like being the one who needs help."

"You think I particularly enjoyed it?"

"You were in trouble so much it was hard to tell."

"Well I'd be home living a pretty damn normal life if not for your drama. That must count for something."

"If there comes a day when you and I are ever bored, just living like normal people do, let's make a pact."

"Okay," Piper hummed skeptically.

"If there comes a day when we're not in some kind of trouble anymore, let's promise we won't go looking for any. We'll just sit in our rocking chairs and enjoy the quiet."

"Deal," Piper mouthed as she backed out of the room and gave Michael a tiny wave. Off his daughter went in the arms of his friend, and at least for tonight, he knew Frankie would be safe and happy.

Chapter Fifteen

Michael dug his fingers deep into the muscle of his neck as he tried to break up the knot that had formed from sleeping on the couch in his father's office. He'd only gotten a couple hours before the sun broke through the window and woke him. He wasn't tired though. There was too much adrenaline pumping through his body to acknowledge his lack of sleep.

Jules and Frankie had both been out cold when he crept in the room, grabbed his clothes and took a quick shower. Now, as he made his way toward the dining room for breakfast, he knew everyone would be up.

"There you are." Jules smiled, and he felt relieved to know his presence still elicited that reaction from her. "Where did you sleep last night?"

"I crashed on the couch in my father's office. I nearly pulled an all-nighter. How about you? You were out late."

Jules strapped Frankie into the highchair and then stared down at her shoes as though guilt were keeping her from looking up. "It was nearly midnight before we came in. I know that's not like me, but I have to tell you, Michael, I really needed a day like that. We went shopping, then the spa, and dinner followed by a drive through town." Michael had to strain to see it, but then he was sure, Jules was crying. Just a subtle couple of tears rolling down her cheek.

"What's the matter?" he asked nervously as he pulled her body against his in a tight hug. Had his mother hurt her? Said something unforgivably rude? He'd lose it on her if that were the case.

100

"I'm so sorry," Jules choked into his shoulder. "I should have told you how I've been feeling lately. I just didn't want you to think any less of me. I didn't want you to confuse my feelings and think I'm not happy being a mom. I'm so happy being a mother, but I need to be more than just one thing. I need to do things like last night and breathe fresh air after nine p.m. I need to talk to other adults and put makeup on and feel like my life is semi-normal again. Does that make me sound selfish?"

"Not at all," Michael assured her as he pulled her back so he could look her square in the eye. "You've been doing so much of this on your own. I'm busy with work, everyone else is doing school or running the restaurant, and I guess I lost sight of how hard this must be for you. Then I go and just bail on you. My timing probably couldn't have been worse." Michael drew in a deep breath as he wondered how his life had gone from a trajectory toward sheer perfection to a rocky, complicated, overgrown mess. "When all this is over and we're home in a few days, I promise to make this right. You deserve time to yourself, time to feel like the old you again."

Jules wiped away the tears as the clamoring voices of the staff entered the room and then instantly silenced at the sight of them.

"We should talk about that, Michael," Jules said as her hand clamped down on his bicep. "I spent a lot of time yesterday with your mother and your sister. I'm not going to oversimplify the issue, but I do think with a little effort we can all come to an understanding."

"Don't do that," Michael said abruptly, pulling his arm away and then regretting the harshness in his voice. "You don't talk like that; those are my mother's words.

You say things like there's no problem that can't be solved with some moonshine and rocking chairs. You are one of the most authentic outspoken women I know; please don't let spending time with her change that. My mother is toxic. She is manipulating you into thinking the problems between us are small. They are not. My mother has two agendas: to stay rich and to keep her image intact. Both of those things are on very thin ice. She'll do anything to protect that. Even—"

"Even be friendly to country folk like me?" Jules asked with an arch of her brows. "How preposterous that she might actually like me because this is more to me than just some cute sayings about sweet tea. Maybe your mother actually thinks I'm worth spending time with and it has nothing to do with whatever drama you two have. I've been pretty quiet since having Frankie. I've been staying up all night and doing everything that needs to be done. I get a say in what we do out here. I have a voice in this. I want to be here for your sister's engagement party and when we leave here I want a plan for how you're going to fix things with your mother so we can all have a relationship. Frankie deserves the best we can give her, and you have to admit that there are things out here we'll never be able to offer her back in Edenville. I want a say in those choices."

Michael felt like he'd just gone ten rounds in the ring with a heavyweight champion. How had his mother worked her dark magic so fast on the woman he loved? But then, wasn't it clear? Jules was telling him how. She'd been feeling overwhelmed by motherhood. She was tired, and he'd abandoned her like a jackass. His mother found every crack in Jules and bled her way in. By the time he found the words he needed, a mix of compassion and begging, it was too late. The dining room came alive with chatter. His mother burst her way in with Lindsey and Piper in tow.

"I hope everyone is ready for a big breakfast," Tabitha sang as she motioned impatiently at the staff to get moving.

"Before we sit down, Mother, there is something we need to do," Michael explained flatly as he finally tore his eyes off his wife.

"Oh, Michael, it can wait—whatever it is. Jules and I have a very long day planned. There is still so much to do for the party. We're going to the venue today and making sure those buffoons don't screw anything up. Then to the florist to make sure the wisteria is as vibrant as I've been promised. We need a hearty breakfast to deal with all that."

"The eggs can wait, the press can't." Michael turned on his heel and headed out the dining room door toward the front of the house. This was the moment he'd been waiting for since he'd hatched this plan yesterday morning. He'd always prided himself on never sinking to his parents' level but now he realized the reason they were always down on that level was because it got shit done.

"What press?" Tabitha asked, unable to fight the draw that his words had created. She was nipping behind him a second later.

"Jules, you come too. This is a family matter." Michael's voice boomed over his shoulder, and he heard his wife's heels clicking against the marble floor as she joined them just in time for him to swing open the front door. Spread across the lawn were a dozen or so reporters and cameramen all clamoring to get the best spot.

Danielle Stewart

"What are you doing?" Tabitha hissed through a fake smile. Strategically, Michael shifted Jules between himself and his mother so there could be no quiet exchanges. This was the ultimate trap for his mother. She'd never tarnish her image in front of this much press. It's a tactic she used dozens of times on Michael over the years.

"So what's all this about, Michael," one of reporters asked in her nasal tone as she fluffed her hair up in the reflection of a nearby news van. "Everyone's set up and ready to roll, so let's hear it."

"I just wanted to thank you all in person for the time and attention you've given to the passing of my father. As you can all imagine it's been a very difficult time for us." Michael watched as the reporters settled into silence and the lights of the cameras came alive. "My family is heartbroken by my father's sudden death. It has truly rocked us to the core. My father was a planner, a brilliant businessman, and incredible politician. His shoes will be impossible to fill. That's the reason I brought you all out here today. As we try to find a way to live in a world without my father, we have to come to terms with the fact that much of what he built can't be sustained without him." Michael paused, mostly for effect but he also wanted to hear if there was anything his mother had to say. He glanced at her briefly from the corner of his eye and found it remarkable how calm she could look when he knew she was raging inside.

"What are you saying, Mr. Cooper?" one of the male reporters asked with furrowed brows as he held the microphone up higher.

"My family needs to grieve and heal right now. We can't dedicate the kind of time, energy, and resources it

104

takes to maintain the work my father was doing. We've made the decision to scale back on everything."

"What do you mean *everything*?" a few of the reporters asked anxiously at once.

"Effective immediately, all charities will be dissolved. The funds will be funneled to the appropriate places and then the paperwork will be filed to close them. The manufacturing business will remain open, but it will be scaled back to just the essentials. No employees will be let go, but the company will run extremely lean."

"You're walking away from your father's legacy? That doesn't seem like a very smart decision." The chatter began to grow, as clearly this was the thought that was ringing through the minds of every reporter on the lawn.

"It isn't a smart decision. It's one we're making with our hearts, not our heads. As you all reported yesterday afternoon, I have a wife and daughter now. I'm older than my father was when he had me, and he spent much of his life working. I don't begrudge him for that because I know it was something he did for us. But after such a loss I'm sure the public will understand why we're making this choice. There is no amount of money or wealth that can give me back my father."

"It's pretty widely known that you haven't had any relationship with your father for almost nine years—since you mysteriously left. It seems strange that you're mourning him now," the nasal and big-haired journalist spoke out brashly.

"There is a vast difference between what is shown in the media and what is real. I didn't splash my relationship with my father across the newspapers; that didn't mean it didn't exist. Things happen every day outside of your view. I buried my father a few days ago, and it has forever changed my life. We've come together as a family and decided to make nothing more important than family."

"Tabitha, these charities have been your whole life for over a decade. You're honestly going to put all that behind you?" the reporter pressed on.

"My mother's whole life is more than the work she's done with charities. Maybe that's the problem. All we're seen as is a culmination of the business decisions we've made over the years. Let this be the one that speaks volumes about us. We will, of course, continue to support and fund charities important to us. We will still employee people who have worked loyally at this company for decades. But we are at a time in our lives where the only thing that matters is our love in this family. I'm sure many of my father's associates will want to discuss this, and I encourage them to contact me. I'll be in my father's office working nonstop to implement the necessary changes. Again, I can't thank the community enough for the outpouring of love and support they've shown to my family during this impossibly hard time. As we go into the weekend we're going to find a way to celebrate even with our heavy hearts. We just ask that you keep us in your prayers." Michael bowed his head and held his breath for a moment, waiting to see if any of the reporters would have anything else to say, but they were seemingly stunned into silence. He fought to not throw his fist in the air in victory. Wrapping one arm around his mother and the other around Jules he moved them back toward the door and gestured for them to head inside.

When the door closed tightly behind them, he was face to face with his mother who transformed quickly into the pit bull he knew she was. Michael was hopeful she'd show her true colors and kill two birds with one stone. Surely if Jules saw his mother's wrath at the idea of losing her fortune everything would become crystal clear.

"How could you do that?" she hissed. A glance in Jules's direction reminded her to force tears. "How could you make the decision without consulting me? The charity work I do means the world to me, and I am not ready to give it up. I know you are angry with me, but do you really hate me so much that in my darkest hour you'd take away anything that makes me happy?" She puffed out some sobs as she steadied herself against the wall.

"Michael, you didn't talk to her about this first?" Jules had a look of horror painted across her face. "All those things you just said out there, they were more lies? You didn't have a relationship with your father. You didn't all come to this agreement together. What are you trying to do?" Jules reached an arm out to a shaking Tabitha, offering her support both physically and emotionally.

"You want the truth?" Michael had reached his max as far as the games Tabitha was playing with his wife's heart. "Those charities are all bogus. They are funnels for laundering money. Don't act as though you're curing cancer and supporting sick kids, Mother."

"I never handled that aspect of the charities, but I fought damn hard to ensure the people who deserved it received funds. I don't condone your father's business practices, but I'm also not going to speak ill of the dead." Tabitha shook her head disgustedly in Michael's direction, laying it all on thick for Jules's benefit.

"Bullshit," Michael bit back and was met with a fake gasp from his mother and a real one from his wife.

"What the hell is wrong with you, Michael?" Jules stepped forward, putting her body between him and his mother like an ill-advised protective shield. "I have never heard you speak to anyone like this, let alone your own mother. You made dramatic and sweeping changes to her livelihood and her passion, and you expect her to just accept that? I feel like you might have gone over the edge or something. I don't even recognize the man in front of me."

"Jules," Michael cut in to explain, but his mother's voice was sharper and beat him to the punch.

"I know you are trying to hurt me. You think I failed you as a mother by not protecting you from your father's greed and bad choices. Maybe that's my cross to bear. I understand that, but scaling back your father's businesses and closing these charities is not the way to get back at me." She raised her hands to her lips to hold back a sob. "I promised your sister I'd get things done for her today, and I can't let her down. Knowing her father's legacy is being destroyed will be hard enough for her to deal with."

"I'm going with you, Tabitha. I'll help anyway I can." Jules smiled warmly as she put an arm around her and patted her back gently.

"Jules, we need to finish this conversation," Michael insisted as Tabitha broke away and shuffled solemnly away from them.

"I don't think this is something we're going to hash out in a few minutes. You had better take a long hard look at yourself and what you're doing just to spite your mother."

"I'm going to finish what I started here with my father's mess in order to protect Josephine from the backlash he set her up to take. Then we'll go to her party and be on a plane that night. We need to get back to our lives and start putting this behind us."

"Putting this behind us? This is your *family*. You can't just cut it off like a limb you can live without. Why are you trying to hurt your mother so badly? She deserves better than to have everything she's worked on taken away from her without so much as a say in the matter."

"She deserves nothing," Michael growled back. "My mother crushes anything on her path to money. She uses and discards people like chess pieces who've served their purpose. That's why we're leaving."

"You don't get to decide when Frankie and I leave. I feel like this place could be the key to her future and you're slamming the door before I even get to peek my head in and look around. That's not fair."

Michael swallowed hard. The idea of Frankie ever growing up here made a knot in his stomach pull tight. "We can give Frankie everything she needs back in Edenville. There is nothing here worth the trouble."

"That's easy for you to say. You grew up here. My mother grew up in a house with dirt floors and cracks so big in the walls that weeds grew in."

"You didn't grow up like that. There is nothing wrong with your house," Michael argued.

"No, my house had running hot water but I was still mucking stalls and doing odd jobs anywhere I could get them to earn money by the time I was ten years old. By fourteen I babysat every weekend to save up for a bike I never bought because my daddy died and I wanted my mom to use the money for bills. And by seventeen I was working at the five and dime and delivering papers in the morning so I could save up for a prom dress that looked a little bit like one I fell in love with in a magazine. I didn't go to the best school; I went to the school closest to my house. A good college was out of the question for me. I want better for my daughter. I want her world to be bigger than just a tiny town with familiar faces."

"We are doing fine right now, Jules. We're not living paycheck to paycheck. There is plenty we'll be able to do for Frankie. I know my mother bought you a fancy dress and said all the right things to you, but you can't fall for that."

"Like I just fell off the turnip truck or something, right? This has nothing to do with a dress or the spa. This is about watching a man I love act like an ass to the person who gave him life. This is about not feeling like I have a voice in my own marriage. I don't want to be told when and where I need to go." Jules let her voice grow harsh, but Michael could tell she was standing on a cliff of tears.

"Can you please just remember how much you love and trust me? Remember our vows. I would never do anything to hurt you or Frankie. If I'm telling you something is toxic, can't you just believe me?" Michael felt a threat of tears himself as he pleaded with his wife.

"I think you are angry. You're judging your mom based on who she was the last time you saw her almost a decade ago. People change. People grow and get better, and it's up to us to give them a chance to prove it."

"Why do you always have to fight me on things?" Michael had to beat back the urge to raise his voice. He knew that wouldn't work with his wife. She never responded well to being told what to do. As matter of fact it usually sent her running in the opposite direction.

"Is it really so impossible to imagine that maybe I'm right about something? When we made those vows you were holding back half of your life. I knew nothing about your family. Maybe if you had told me from the beginning, we wouldn't be in this situation in the first place. You left me, you lied to me, and you didn't trust me enough to help you. Did we give up on Willow when she thought she was running away for her own good? Did we let Piper run off on her own to face her family? We're supposed to do these things together, but you act like you're an island. Like you don't need anybody. We can do this together but you have to value my opinion. You haven't seen your mom in a long time, but you're acting like you know exactly why she does what she does."

"I'm judging my mom based on precedents and history. It would be foolish of me to think she's changed. I have too much to lose. People like that don't change. Yes we chased after Willow and we stood by Piper but that's apples and oranges. Trusting my mom would be as stupid as believing the man who hunted Piper down had changed over the years."

"I guess I'm just that kind of stupid then, because I look at your mother and I think of my mother when she lost her husband. It's devastating. She needs you."

"I can't think of two more polar opposites in the world than my mother and Betty. They have nothing in common. My mother isn't mourning the loss of the man she loved—they *hated* each other. They had a mutually beneficial relationship that served a purpose. There was no love or respect or even fidelity between them. My mother is mourning the loss of her bankroll, not her husband. She and Betty have *nothing* in common." Michael felt blood rushing to his face. It was an insult to Betty to ever be compared to a woman like his mother.

"I'm going with her today because I promised to help her. The rest we'll need to take day by day. I don't have a good solution for the two of you, but I'm not going to stop trying to find one. She's your mother, Michael; don't give up on her. I don't think she's given up on you."

"The only person I care about not giving up on me is you. You're the only thing in my life that matters to me. If I have you and Frankie that's all I need."

"It's not like we have a huge family, Michael. Who does Frankie really have? It's just my mom back in Edenville."

"How can you say that?" Michael's voice was booming now and he could do little to rein it in. "We have Bobby and Piper. We have Jedda and Clay and Crystal. Hell we even have Willow—she's like the crazy aunt. Just because they're not blood doesn't mean they're not our family. And just because these people here are, doesn't mean we should trust them."

"And just because the road has been bumpy in the past doesn't mean it can't smooth out in the future. All I'm asking is that you give your mother a chance because I intend to. I hope one day when Frankie gets older if I'm ever in this position with her she'll give me that chance." Jules gestured toward the dining room where her daughter was sitting with Piper.

"You are ten times the mother my mother is. You will never be in a situation like this with our daughter. You'll never need that second chance. And in my case, I've given my mother a *hundred* chances."

"So maybe she needs one more. What do you have to lose?"

"You."

Chapter Sixteen

"I feel like we missed something," Piper said as she sidled up to Michael and nudged him out of his frustrated trance. Watching Jules storm off to find his mother had his skin feeling like it had been raked over with hot barbed wire.

"You did," he explained as he scooped Frankie up into his arms and squeezed her tight. "Did she eat a good breakfast?"

"She didn't seem very hungry this morning. I don't know why. I'll give her a bottle in a little bit and see how she does."

"No, I need you to go with Jules today. I completely blindsided my mother by telling her in front of the press I'm closing down all my father's charities and scaling his business down dramatically."

"She must have flipped," Lindsey said with wide eyes.

"My mother is a professional. She has quite the poker face. It's why I did it in front of the media like that. I knew she wouldn't fly off the handle, even though what I was saying would drive her insane. And she's trying to preserve her reputation with Jules so she'll hold back there, too. But I need you with her today. All day. No exceptions. My mother will have her ear, and she'll be trying to plant little seeds to get her way."

"I'm not sure Jules will listen to me. I pushed yesterday and it only got between us."

"I know. Jules doesn't like people telling her what's for her own good. So just be with her. Listen to what my mother is saying and fill me in on what her angle seems to be. I don't know how she's going to try to force me to change my mind, but I know she will. Right now my only weakness is my family, and she won't hesitate to find a way to keep us here long enough for me to go back on what I said."

"What can we do to help?" Lindsey asked as she folded her arms across her chest and her face fell serious, clearly ready for marching orders.

"I could use some help here. I just announced to all my father's associates that their laundering and back-room deals are coming to an end. There will be plenty of people besides my mother who will be unhappy enough about this to try to do something. I expect the phone calls and in-person meetings to start any minute. I could use some help building profiles and digging into everyone. Who has the most to lose and who is most likely to try to strike back at me?"

"Sure, I can play detective for the day. I was getting antsy here just eating fancy French toast and waiting for something to happen. But I don't understand why you don't just turn everything over to the appropriate authorities. It doesn't seem like your goal is to protect your father's reputation. Why not just walk away?"

"My father betrayed my sister and used her name to carry on enough illegal activities she'd face jail time if they come out. I don't trust my mother to have the desire or skill to protect Jo. She's too greedy to care what happens to her. My father tried to do the same thing to me years ago. It's why I left. I just want to spare my sister from having to pay for his crimes. She doesn't deserve that. The only way I can think to do that is to close everything down and bury what I can. With any luck no one will dig too deep."

"That's a tough spot to be in. What does your sister think of all this?" Lindsey asked, already in detective mode.

"She doesn't know anything about it. She thinks my father was an upstanding guy who was teaching her the ropes of the business. She doesn't know that every document she signed and every deposit she made was getting her deeper and deeper in trouble. I'd like to get most of this resolved before I let her in on it. She's excited to start her life and be married; I don't want her worrying about this stuff."

I'll grab my laptop and meet you in your office."

"It's not my office. It's my father's and every time I sit in there I hate it even more."

Lindsey shrugged her shoulders and jogged off toward the room she was staying in to retrieve her things.

"What about Frankie? I don't like leaving her here all day with a nanny. It doesn't feel right. Especially if you're worried about what your mother may do." Piper swept one of Frankie's growing red curls away from her eyes.

"My mother is a lot of things, but she wouldn't hurt Frankie. Nicolette has been with our family for ages and practically raised my sister. I'll have Lindsey check in throughout the day. I just need you thinking of a way to keep Jules from completely falling for my mother's shit and forgetting that I do the things I do to keep her safe."

"I'm supposed to do all that without saying anything?" Piper raised a skeptical eyebrow at him.

"I didn't say I knew how you were going to do it, just that I need you to. You know Jules as well as anyone. Just think of what normally makes her come to her senses."

"I have one trick up my sleeve." Piper grinned as she headed back toward the dining room and blew a kiss to Frankie before disappearing.

Michael closed his eyes and kissed the crown of his daughter's head. "We just need to get out of here and back to Edenville. Then everything can go back to normal. Well, as normal as you can call it when your Grandma Betty is around."

Danielle Stewart

Chapter Seventeen

"Jules, please wait up," Piper called as she sped up to catch Jules and Tabitha before they could disappear into the waiting car.

"Piper, you don't need to come with us today. Tabitha has been through enough, and she's just trying to finish up the details for the engagement party." Jules lowered her voice as she leaned in toward Piper who'd finally reached them. "She doesn't need you having a bad attitude about everything and defending Michael's absolutely selfish choices today."

"I'm not going to. Michael told me what happened, and I just want to be with you and make sure you're okay. I promise I won't have an attitude or even interject my opinion at all."

"But you do have an opinion and you're on Michael's side," Jules said, raising her brows up defiantly.

"I don't know enough about any of it to even have an opinion. You're my best friend, and you've always stood by me. I just want to be with you today, and I don't care about anyone else's drama."

"Are you going to make me feel terrible about not having Frankie with me today? I'm not crazy about leaving her again, but Tabitha really needs the company. You should have seen it this morning. It was awful to watch."

"Frankie is with Nicolette, and Lindsey will be checking in too. She'll be fine. Just let me come with you. Please."

"Fine," Jules relented, gesturing for Piper to get in.

118

"Where are we off to first?" Piper asked, trying to sound bubbly and excited for whatever tedious task lay before them.

"You're coming?" Tabitha asked with a look like she suddenly smelled something unsavory.

"I'm looking forward to helping with the party details. It's not something I've ever done before. So where do we start?"

"We're meeting my daughter at the venue to make sure everything is on track for the party in two days. I'm sure by now she's heard the news, though. She won't likely be able to even focus on the party. She'll be devastated."

"I know, Tabitha. I can't imagine what you're going through right now. No one would blame you if you stayed home today and just processed the changes." Jules patted Tabitha's shoulder, which was rigid with anger.

"I have no intention of processing anything. He is not taking away everything I have worked hard for over the years. If he thinks I'm just going to lie down and take this because he's upset at his father, he has another think coming."

"But everything is in his name, isn't it? It's his legal decision to do whatever he wants with the businesses and charities. Why would your husband do that if they weren't speaking?"

"The will hasn't been updated since before Michael moved away. There was a time when they were so close, and it was in the plans for Michael to take over everything. Once they had a falling out his father always hoped Michael would come back and things could go back to normal. I will tell you one thing, my husband never intended for Michael to dismantle his legacy and leave me and Josephine with nothing."

"Why did Michael leave in the first place?" Piper asked. Jules wanted to snap at her for getting involved, but she actually wanted to know the answer too, so she stayed silent and waited.

"Because that's what fathers and sons do," Tabitha snapped back. "They were more alike than either of them would admit, and because of that, they didn't agree on much."

"What do you intend to do to keep Michael from moving forward with his plans? It sounds like he's already got the ball rolling on most of it." Piper shifted in her seat slightly and Jules could tell her friend was working another agenda. But again, Jules wanted an answer to the question.

"The only thing that will change his mind is seeing himself as part of this family and believing he could have a future here in Ohio again, at least in some capacity. Right now he's just trying to get through the weekend and then leave us here like we're strangers. If he stayed a little longer and saw Josephine and me as something other than just the wife and daughter of a man he hated, maybe he could stop making decisions out of spite and anger. He doesn't want the burden of continuing his father's legacy, and in the process he's destroying our lives. I know he's not that kind of man, but right now he's making it hard to remember the sweet boy he once was. Does he intend to keep Frankie from me? Does he intend to never see me again after this?" Tabitha broke into a sob and covered her face with her hands as her shoulders shook.

"No," Jules said adamantly. "He will not keep Frankie from you. I won't let that happen. We don't have much family, and I'm not going to let him just cut you out of her life like that. You are her grandmother and you have the right to see her whenever you want."

"I know if you leave after this party I'll never have the chance to make any of this right," Tabitha choked out.

"I've already told him he doesn't get to decide when Frankie and I leave. He's my husband, not my keeper. I honestly can't believe how he's acting. I've never known him to make decisions just to spite people."

"Neither have I," Piper cut in. "He always has a reason for what he does. He's very calculated and levelheaded."

"Usually, yes. But the way I've seen him acting here is frightening. I don't intend to just run off to Edenville and pretend none of this ever happened."

"So you're going to stay here?" Piper asked, and Jules knew her well enough to see she was fighting back her own opinion in the matter.

"Oh, please tell me you are staying. I can't imagine losing everything in one week. My husband, our livelihood, and my grandchild. I won't survive all of that." Tabitha clutched at Jules's leg desperately.

"I don't know, really," Jules explained, now feeling like it would be wrong to promise something she really wasn't entirely sure about yet. Wouldn't false hope be worse than leaving? All she had meant was that Michael wasn't the decision-maker for the entire family. "I just want you to know that I'll talk to Michael and try to understand more of what is going on. I feel like we've hardly had a chance to talk since all this started. I'm sure I can get through to him."

Like a hot air balloon whose flame had been extinguished, Tabitha shriveled and shrank. Jules hadn't given her the exact answers she'd been looking for.

The car slowed to a stop in front of a large museum-like building before Tabitha could voice her apparent disappointment and concern. At the top of the grand front steps stood Josephine, wearing a gray designer pantsuit and a scowl. Jules felt a rock sinking in her stomach at the idea of having to face another person Michael had blindsided with the news this morning. Her anger at him was growing, but like a small fractal of light cutting through that darkness there was a part of her that wondered why a man who always acted with logic and forethought would now make rash and spiteful decisions. And the answer in her head kept ringing the same: *he wouldn't.*

Chapter Eighteen

Josephine had requested a moment alone with her mother, and the two stepped inside a small office while Jules and Piper headed into the large ballroom where the party would be held.

"I feel terrible," Jules said as she bit down on her nails and then stopped suddenly when she remembered how much the deluxe manicure had cost Tabitha. "I don't understand why Michael is doing this. Just because he can shut everything down doesn't mean he should. We could make things work out here."

"Are you saying you want to stay in Ohio?" Piper asked, unable to hide her concern at that idea.

"No, I'm saying it wouldn't be impossible to spend some time out here and some in Edenville. Michael could run everything and not uproot their lives completely the way he is. Tabitha loves these charities. I know they aren't completely clean of any corruption, but she's had nothing to do with that. She shouldn't be punished for her husband's mistakes."

"I'm sure it'll all work out," Piper said noncommittally, looking around the large room to avoid eye contact with Jules.

"Really, you're going with that for an answer?"

"I told you I'd come out with you today and not interject my opinion. I'm just trying to be supportive."

"Well, stop it for a minute and just tell me what you really think."

"I think you're stating things as fact when you aren't really positive. You don't know if Tabitha had nothing to do with the corruption of those charities. You're giving her undue trust, and in the process you're showing Michael you don't trust him."

"And what if Michael is just angry and acting like a stupid jerk because he's mad? Do they deserve that? I'm not ready to tell them to stay out of our lives."

"I've never known him to make decisions based solely on emotions. That's kind of your department." Piper smiled slightly but quickly tucked it away.

"What do you think I should do? And don't tell me to trust Michael." Jules bit nervously at her lip and glanced over her shoulder to see if Tabitha and Josephine were coming.

"I don't think you should do anything. Don't promise to stay and don't plan on leaving. Give it all a little more time. Talk to Michael, and give him a chance to explain. I'm not saying to blindly trust him, I'm saying listen to what he has to say."

"Is she telling you to listen to what Michael has to say? Isn't that sage advice?" Tabitha asked as she suddenly appeared out of nowhere with Josephine by her side and startled them.

"Tabitha, this isn't an easy time for any of us. I certainly never thought I'd be in the middle of something like this by coming out here." Jules felt sweat begin to bead on the back of her neck at the idea of having a confrontation with Tabitha.

Looking as though she were an overfull volcano about to spew lava, Tabitha turned a new shade of red. But then as quick as the wave came, it seemed to subside. "I understand. This really isn't easy for any of us. I'm afraid now, that's all. I don't want to lose you and Frankie. Michael doesn't have a reason to run anymore, so I hope he doesn't."

Tabitha pulled Jules in for a tight hug and patted her back gently. Jules felt the weight of the world come off her shoulders. She thought for sure Tabitha was about to flip out on her. But she didn't. Crisis averted.

"Now, this day is about Josephine. So let's get down to business, making sure this event is perfect." Tabitha turned toward her daughter and gently touched her cheek.

"Thank you, Mother," Josephine said with a smile. "I'm sorry you're in the middle of this, Jules. I've always wanted a sister and I can see you and I have so much in common. I hope that we can make this all work somehow."

"I hope so too," Jules said, wiping away a tear and pulling Josephine in for a hug.

As Tabitha and Josephine stepped away to get the attention of the party planner who'd walked in, Piper leaned in toward Jules.

"I know that look. You are planning something," Piper whispered.

"There has to be a way to work all of this out."

Piper rolled her eyes and shook her head at Jules. "Just be careful."

"My middle name is careful." Jules grinned at her best friend.

"No, you're middle name is Marie, and you're never careful."

Chapter Nineteen

"You've got to be kidding with this shit, Michael," Tim Abraham, his father's point person in overseas purchases for the manufacturing business, barked as he charged into the office and closed the door tightly behind him.

"It's not a joke. I'm shutting everything down. You'll have to launder your money somewhere else."

"Your father would roll over in his grave if he knew what a pussy you were being," Tim retorted as he slammed his pudgy fist down on the desk. His wispy gray combover seemed to be glowing against his crimson face.

"There isn't room for debate here, Tim. I've got the majority of the paperwork ready to be filed. It's done. Now let's talk about what that means for you. By scaling back the manufacturing company significantly we won't be sourcing as heavily from outside the United States anymore. Your services won't be necessary." Michael leaned back in his chair and crossed his arms over his chest the way his father used to do.

"How about I just gather up some reporters and let them know about the deal your father had with a fabric company in Taiwan? He had a lot of blood on his hands after that."

Michael took in the smug look on Tim's round face as he shuffled the papers on his desk until the one with Tim's name was on the top. "It's interesting you know so much about that deal. It's likely because you helped broker it. Cy Hue seems to have made quite a few calls to your office over the last six months. And the wire transfer of forty thousand dollars he sent you, was that a birthday present?" Michael said a silent thank you to Lindsey's awesome detective work for setting this up so perfectly.

The haughty look of victory dropped from Tim's face and was replaced with a worried one. "What are you, some kind of private investigator now or something? I don't suppose you had a warrant to find all that."

"No, I'm a lawyer who has every intention of getting my family out of this shit and going back to my life. I'm not here to turn people in. Your crimes die with my father's as far as I'm concerned. But you need to find a new partner in crime. I'm sure all my father's other associates will be looking to start over with someone else. This could actually be a good opportunity for you too."

Tim leaned back on his heels as he considered what was being said. His hand ran thoughtfully under one of his chins. "Will you put my name out there to anyone you think might be interested in striking a deal?"

"Fine," Michael shrugged, seeing no harm in connecting one bad person to another. They'd find each other eventually anyway, but at least this way they'd have less motivation to come after the Cooper family.

"Not everyone is going to be as easy to convince as I am. I happen to have very diverse partnerships out there. It's the people who worked exclusively with your father that will have the most to lose."

"Thanks, I'll keep that in mind," Michael said hollowly as he gestured toward the door. When it shut behind Tim, Michael let out a tired sigh and allowed himself a brief moment of rest. He and Lindsey had already spent the morning going over which of his father's associates had the most to lose and whose hands were the dirtiest. Michael was carefully prepared for each meeting. As the phone on his father's desk rang again, he forced his tired eyes open and drew in a deep breath.

"Michael Cooper," he grumbled as he put the receiver to his ear.

"That was some show you put on this morning," a woman's voice hummed on the other end of the line. "I'm Clara Epstein."

Clara was enemy number one on the list he and Lindsey had created. She was a relatively squeaky clean politician, if there was such a thing, who'd begun working with his father a few months ago. On paper he was funding part of her campaign, but in reality he was doing much more. He'd begun advocating on her behalf behind closed doors and swapping favors for votes. The problem, besides being unethical and illegal, was Clara had kept herself completely clear of any wrongdoing as far as Michael could tell. For some reason his father was helping Clara, but there didn't seem to be anything given to him in return. No money. No real estate, nothing passed between them that could be tracked as payment.

Since he didn't have an answer he'd play dumb. "Hello Mrs. Epstein. What can I do for you today?"

"Your father and I had an arrangement. I'd like to make an appointment with you today to discuss it in person." Her voice was level and professional, but Michael could sense the edge of nerves as well.

"That would be fine. I'm available all day today. When would you like to stop by?" Before she could answer Michael heard a light tap on the door that slowly grew louder. "One moment please, Clara."

The office door cracked open and Nicolette peeked her head in timidly. "I'm so sorry to interrupt, Mr.

Cooper. I tried to reach Mrs. Cooper on the phone but couldn't. It's the baby."

Without a thought about the woman waiting on hold on the phone Michael shot to his feet and started heading toward the nursery. "What is it? What happened?"

"She's not eating and she's sleeping most of the day. She's very warm. I was just going to take her temperature but I wanted to let you know first." Nicolette spoke frantically, matching the way Michael was feeling.

"I'll call Jules and tell her to come home. We need to take her to the doctor. I don't know any doctors out here. Who do we call?" He fumbled his cell phone out of his pocket.

"I'll call Dr. Sans. He was your sister's pediatrician, and I know he lives close by. He used to make house calls back when your sister had her stomach problems. If he can come maybe we shouldn't bother your wife. Not until he has a chance to see the baby. It may be nothing."

"I . . ." Michael thought it over. Jules would not want to be the last to know if something was wrong with Frankie. But she may also assume he was being an alarmist just to cut her day short with his mother. "If he can get here quickly then I'll wait."

Within twenty minutes the thin, beak-nosed doctor was hustling into the nursery where Michael was rocking his sleepy daughter.

"Thank you for coming on such short notice."

"Can you tell me when the symptoms started?" Dr. Sans asked as he pulled a stethoscope out of his bag.

"I'm not sure. I've been so focused on my father's business I haven't spent much time with her." Michael turned toward Nicolette, hoping she could shed some light.

Danielle Stewart

"She ate very well yesterday at lunch and was awake and alert this morning. But sometime after breakfast she started getting fussy, sleepy, and wouldn't eat. I thought maybe she was just teething, but she's been sleeping since breakfast and doesn't want to wake up for much longer than a few minutes here and there."

"That's not like her at all. She hates sleeping. She hardly ever sleeps during the day, other than one nap in the afternoon. Even at night she's still up a few times." Michael felt an ache in his heart for Jules. He'd been taking for granted how little sleep she had been getting and had overlooked how overwhelmed she was feeling. He should have been getting up more to help her at night. He'd been so selfish. He knew her inability to nurse had been eating at her too. Pumping and bottle-feeding had not been in her original plan. It all felt like it was finally sinking in for him about how hard Jules's job really was these days.

"Any allergies?" he asked as he gestured for Michael to shift Frankie in his arms so he could examine her better.

"None that we know of so far. She had some reflux as a baby but it's been better since we started solid foods about a month ago."

After a quick examination the doctor began shaking his head and jotting some notes down in a pad he had tucked back in his pocket. "It looks like she has a double ear infection. I'm shocked she's sleeping. She should be in quite a bit of pain. She's a tough little girl. That would account for the lack of appetite and being so tired. Her eardrums are very inflamed and even if we put her on antibiotics they still might burst over the next day or so. I'll call in a prescription you can pick up tonight."

"What does that mean? Her ear drums might burst, that sounds serious." Michael instantly wished Jules was here now.

"It really isn't. It happens more than you would think, and if they burst it will actually relieve the pressure she's feeling. They'll heal on their own with time. She'll just need to be watched closely. She has a slight fever now. You can give her something for it, and if it gets higher than one hundred three please call me right away."

"But she's not eating; that seems pretty dangerous. Shouldn't we be worried about that?" Michael asked nervously.

"Make sure she gets some fluids. If her eyes look sunken or she goes longer than six hours without a wet diaper, then call me for that as well. I know it seems very frightening, but many kids get ear infections. It's important we stay on top of it. I'm just around the corner so you can call me anytime. Your mother and I go back many years. I'm happy to help. I'll come back tomorrow morning to check either way."

"Thank you, Doctor. I really appreciate it."

Dr. Sans quietly slipped out of the room followed by Nicolette, who would see him out of the house. As Frankie shifted slightly in Michael's arms he sank back into the rocking chair and let her curl comfortably into him. He hoped she couldn't feel the shaking in his legs or his heart thumping in his chest. He hadn't cried since the day she was born, but now he felt a tear blazing its way down his cheek. Frankie and Jules were his entire world. He prayed there would never be a moment of his life spent without them.

He shifted slightly and fished his phone out of his pocket. Sending a text message to Jules to come home, he knew his wife well enough to know nothing would matter except the health of their child. They would put aside everything and everyone to make sure Frankie was all right.

Chapter Twenty

"Where is she?" Jules stammered as she practically fell through the front door.

"Michael is in rocking her right now. He hasn't left her side since the doctor came in," Nicolette explained as she ushered them back toward the nursery.

"I'm sure she's fine," Tabitha comforted as she quickened her pace to stay by Jules's side, elbowing Piper away slightly. "Dr. Sans is a family friend. He'll be at our beck and call whenever we need him. And we paid for an entire wing at Cincinnati Children's Hospital so we have access to any kind of specialist you can imagine."

"Michael said it's an ear infection. Those are pretty common, aren't they?" Piper asked, clearly trying to make a point.

"When it comes to my granddaughter we certainly won't be taking any chances. She'll have the best care available to her. Ear infections might be common, but we won't be treating them like they are." Tabitha pushed open the door to the nursery and when the light cut into the room Jules caught a glimpse of Michael's weary face.

"How is she?" Jules asked, racing to his side and dropping to her knees next to the rocking chair.

"She's fussing a bit and then groggy. I tried to give her a bottle, but she won't take it. Maybe she will take it from you." The desperation in her husband's eyes tugged at her already fragile heart.

Jules stood and opened her arms and Michael looked relieved to have his other half there to help. As Frankie sank into her arms she could feel something was different. Her daughter was the kind of child who stirred at any sound and awoke from the slightest movement.

133

This child in her arms was out cold. Her fluttering little eyelashes and tiny snores were not comforting—for a child like Frankie they were frightening.

Michael handed the bottle over as Jules lowered herself to the rocking chair. The doorway was full of concerned heads but the light streaming in from the hallway wasn't helping. "Could you guys give us a minute to try to feed her?" Jules asked, and Michael practically shoved everyone out the door and closed it tight.

"I'm sorry I was gone. I should have been here," Jules apologized as she eased the bottle into Frankie's mouth and moved it against her three teeth and little gums to get her to latch onto it. Though it took a few tries eventually she began to take in a few sips and then, like she did at every feeding, Frankie tangled her little fingers up into Jules's flowing red hair. There were some nights the endless tugging on her hair would drive Jules crazy, but tonight it brought tears to her eyes.

Michael pulled the large plush chair in the corner over to the side of the rocking chair. He slid his arm behind Jules's head and rubbed her shoulder. "I was really scared," he whispered, his voice shaking.

"I'm sorry we've been fighting," Jules sighed, leaning her tired head on his shoulder. "Nothing is more important to me than Frankie. We can work anything out."

"I'm sorry too. I've been distracted and caught up in a lot of anger instead of taking the time to talk to you and really explain things. I just kept thinking I could fix all this, and we could go back to our lives, but I can see now I can't do anything unless we're doing it together. You're my partner for a reason. We have gone through so much together, and this should be no different."

"Listening isn't my strong suit but I promise to really hear what you have to say. Let's just get Frankie feeling better, and I know we can work everything else out."

"Look, she took four ounces. That's a good sign. When Nicolette took her temperature a little while ago it was around one hundred one. We'll just need to keep checking it until morning."

"I'll stay with her. I know you have a lot of work to do. Then we can switch after dinner."

"Are you sure? I don't want you to get overwhelmed."

"I'm positive. You couldn't pry her away from me now if you wanted to. I just want to hold her and watch her sleep."

Michael stood and kissed his wife on the top of her red hair and then did the same to his daughter. As she watched her husband leave she closed her eyes and began to hum the same song her mother used to hum to her when Jules was sick. It was something she thought she'd long forgotten, but this afternoon, as she sat rocking her baby in the dark, the tune came right back to her.

Chapter Twenty-One

"Shit." Michael looked down at the phone in his office and remembered the call he'd been on when he learned Frankie was sick. He'd put Clara Epstein on hold and then had never come back. That was over two hours ago. If he'd hoped to tactfully navigate a solution with Clara, leaving her hanging on the line wasn't a good way to start.

He flipped through his papers and dialed her number, hoping she'd still take his call. When it went to voicemail he thumped his palm to his forehead.

"You look like you're having a hell of a day." A woman's voice drew his attention and startled him almost off the edge of his father's leather chair.

"Can I help you?" he asked with an attitude, as he looked up and down the polished woman. Her pencil skirt and pristine pink button-down blouse looked as though they'd been starched ten times over. Her blond hair was styled high and hair sprayed into submission.

"Well you had me on hold so long I thought I'd better come and do a welfare check to make sure you didn't pass out or something. Now looking at you, I'm still wondering if I should call a doctor."

"Clara," Michael said, shooting to his feet. "I'm very sorry about that. My daughter got sick all of the sudden and I panicked."

"Is she all right?" Clara asked. Michael took comfort that her concern seemed completely genuine.

"She'll be fine. Just an ear infection we're watching closely. It was rude of me to leave you on the line. Thank you for coming in." Michael gestured for her to sit down in the chair across from his desk. She took a seat and smoothed her skirt, though no wrinkles had formed.

"The rumor is you're in the process of severing all your father's ties with any associates or business partners." Clara kept her face level and Michael could tell she was trying to read his reaction.

"The rumors are true. I have no intention of staying here in Ohio. There won't be anyone to carry on my father's business, so I'm scaling everything back."

"It sounded more like you are shutting everything down. Your father was incredibly diverse in his partnerships. I'd imagine I'm not the first person at your door with concerns." Clara crossed her legs and rested her chin in her hand as she scrutinized Michael's face some more.

"I do see that my father was a big contributor to your campaign. More than that, it looks as if he was pulling quite a few strings to make sure you got elected. Though I can't figure out why."

"Perhaps your father just agreed with my platform. Maybe he believed in what I stand for." Clara raised an eyebrow, goading him on.

"My father didn't believe in anything except money. The problem is, I can't see any monetary reward for all the work he's done for you. Which means you're trading with some other kind of currency." The code talk was for her benefit. Michael had no problem calling his father greedy and criminal. But he knew a politician would need this conversation to be more tactful.

"And if you were taking some guesses what would you come up with?"

"Well it wasn't sex. You certainly weren't sleeping together."

"And what makes you so sure about that?" Clara had a look of surprise and indignation come over her face.

"I mean this solely as an insult to my father, not toward you. You're too old for him. He likes his mistresses in their twenties. So if this wasn't an affair and it wasn't for monetary gain, why would my father work to get you elected? I've read your platform. You and he are like oil and water. You want to close loopholes he wants to take advantage of them. If anything, you getting elected would be bad for him."

"You've put quite a bit of thought into this. I'm interested in what your hypothesis really is. You crossed a lot off the list. What's left?"

"Blackmail. I'm guessing you came across something on my father and because you're squeaky clean he had nothing to counter with." Michael tapped his pen against the desk and waited for her reply, but the look on her face told him he guessed correctly.

"I certainly didn't go looking for a way to blackmail your father. He was just the kind of man who makes it easy. So now I'm wondering, what do we do from here?"

"I'm in no position to continue supporting your campaign. I'm severing all ties with anyone my father did business with. I have nothing to offer you. If you choose to leak whatever information you have about my father I can't stop you. And I actually don't care. If he was sleeping with somebody, expose her. If he betrayed somebody then put it out there. I'm not here to fight his battles." Michael had perfected his poker face over the years. It's a prerequisite for a lawyer. Today it was getting good use.

"Are you truly trying to lead people to believe you're walking away from this empire your father has left in your lap?"

"The man didn't leave me an empire. He left me a mess. I don't want the money and I don't want the trouble that comes with it. I am not my father. You can't blackmail me and you can't pressure me."

"Why?"

"Do you know where I live? This sleepy little town in North Carolina. Every Wednesday I go to my mother-in-law's house and eat the best dinner in the world. After that I sit on the porch with my wife and best friends and watch the sunset. It is the most incredible calm you've ever experienced in your entire life. I'm a lawyer there. Some days I work on cases about livestock. And that's fine by me. There is nothing my father's money could buy that could make me as happy as I am in North Carolina."

"Do you know what's strange about that?"

"I'd imagine for a politician with built-in narcissism there would be a lot strange about that."

"Actually, what's strange about it is that I believe you. It's been so long since I have believed anyone about anything. I want to get elected so I can stop men like your father. Blackmailing him wasn't my idea, but it worked. I'm well on my way to getting elected now. But I don't have any intention of carrying on through you." Clara pulled a small flash drive from her bag and slid it across the desk toward Michael. "This is everything I have on your father. I'll be honest, it's some pretty ugly stuff. There are no other copies. Just destroy this one and you and I can go our separate ways."

Danielle Stewart

"You are really going to just hand back this enormous bargaining chip? That doesn't seem like something a politician would do."

"I'm not trying to just be a politician. I'm hoping to be a good person. I don't know when those things stop being synonymous, but that's not the world I want to live in. I hope you get back on that plane to North Carolina sooner rather than later. I know plenty of people who had the intention of walking away from a life like this but never got the chance. Something always gets in the way."

"Thank you, Clara. I hope you win the election. This place needs some change."

As Clara stood, Michael did as well. She headed for the door and, as though she was having second thoughts, she glanced over her shoulder. "There is one more thing, Michael. Your mother—she's a crazy person. Your father was a greedy criminal, but your mother is something else entirely. I find her far more dangerous."

Chapter Twenty-Two

The tap on the office door was followed by it's abrupt opening. Michael assumed another annoyed business associate would be storming in, but instead it was his mother.

"We need to talk," she demanded as she closed the door behind her. She didn't make a move to sit, and Michael didn't make a move to stand.

"I don't think we have much to talk about. You asked me to protect Jo. That's what I'm doing."

"No, you're dismantling everything your father and I built, and I'm not going to sit back and let that happen. If you've learned anything about me over the years, Michael, I would hope it would be you don't want a war with me."

"So I guess I should take that as my answer. You couldn't care less about Josephine staying out of jail. This is all about money for you. If I had even the slightest doubt you cared about anything or anyone other than yourself I can put that behind me now. So if there is nothing else . . ." Michael said as he gestured toward the door.

"You're being a fool. Your father had everything lined up and all you had to do is come in here and find a way to keep it going. You weren't even supposed to be in the will. Everything was supposed to be left to me, but that's just one more way your father screwed me over. I'm telling you for the last time, stop what you're trying to do and find a way to keep everything just how it is or you'll regret it for the rest of your life."

"Threats? That's where we're at in this? You give me the steely look and tell me you'll destroy me if I don't bend to your will. The problem with that, Mother, is I don't need anything from you, so what can you withhold? I don't have any skeletons in my closet for you to exploit or blackmail me with. I'm filing the rest of the documents in the next two days and launching the restructuring of the manufacturing company. While it won't be anywhere near the cash flow you're accustomed to, I do intend to turn it all over to you. I'll structure it in a way that requires little intervention on your part, but you can continue to reap the benefits of any profits. Between that and the life insurance, along with some lifestyle changes, you could live out the rest of your life very comfortably."

"You have it all figured out then, don't you? If you're foolish enough to believe you have nothing to lose then you're not nearly the man I thought you were."

"We're staying for this party. I'm tying up every loose end here and then we're leaving. Before this meeting I thought maybe there was a chance that you and I could come to some kind of agreement about managing our relationship so you could be apart of my daughter's life. Now I'm more confident than ever that leaving here is the best choice I ever made, and making it again is easy."

"I don't think you've met half of your father's associates yet, Michael. Maybe you've gotten lucky so far, but they won't all be so willing to walk away."

"They'll all walk away, because there won't be anything left here for them to fight for. You need to come to terms with that. Start looking at your assets and figure out what to liquidate. Don't put your energy into stopping the inevitable."

Michael sat a moment in his father's chair as his mother huffed her way out of the office. He wasn't being honest with himself. He was acting as though he had no concerns about his mother being able to do anything to stop him. The problem with his mother was she'd do just that, *anything.*

Chapter Twenty-Three

Jules closed the door to the nursery gingerly, trying to make sure that a sleeping Frankie stayed that way. Though judging how she'd been acting the last few hours, a marching band could come through and not wake her baby. That was what was so scary. She didn't want to leave her daughter's side, but Michael had insisted he take a shift with her too. When he cradled his daughter in his arms, holding her close as they swayed in the rocking chair, Jules knew they'd be fine together for a little while. She was starving and her shoulders were getting sore. Frankie had taken a few ounces of milk twenty minutes ago, so if Jules were going to take a break, now would be the time. It was just about dinnertime and she was ready to stretch her legs.

"I'm sorry, Josephine," Jules heard Tabitha explain into the phone as she rounded the corner and surprised her. "I have to go." She hung up abruptly and hiccupped a tiny cry.

"Is everything all right?" Jules asked, touching Tabitha's shoulder gently. "I know this has been one hell of a day."

"I'm letting my daughter down, and it's killing me. The party is in two days and I'm far from ready. Right now I'm supposed to be in Chef Corbin's kitchen sampling food options. If I miss this appointment he'll cancel. He's very fickle like that. I'll never be able to find someone else on such short notice."

"Is it too late to make it to the appointment?"

"No, but I'm a mess I can't go over there alone like this. Every time I think about the state of things I burst into tears. I'm shaking like a leaf. Josephine has worked hard her whole life; she just lost her father not long before her wedding. She'll have no one to give her away. She deserves the best engagement party I can provide her, but I'm failing her."

"I guess I could go with you, as long as it will be quick. I'm starving anyway and told Michael I was going to get something to eat. He said not to come back for a couple hours so that I could get a good break. Would that make it easier?"

"You truly are a wonderful person, Jules. I can see why Michael married you. I feel like you're going to be the key to getting this family back together." Tabitha smoothed Jules's crimson locks as she looked at her affectionately.

Jules wondered if the gut-wrenching conflict she was feeling was visible on her face. She had wanted to be the person to help bring Michael and his mother back together. What a hero that would make her. She thought back on all the things Michael had done for her over the years; this would be her way to pay him back. The problem was it had become abundantly clear Michael didn't want a path back to his mother. He wanted a one-way ticket away from her. Jules's meddling and cheerleading for a resolution wasn't helping anything. It had put a wedge between them. Michael had an image of his mother that seemed very different than the impression Jules had gotten. Wasn't that because it was outdated? They'd gone nearly a decade without interacting very much. His anger was misdirected. Surely his father was the intended target; his mother was just the closest target. She bit at her lip as she thought how to answer Tabitha's statement.

"I hope things do work out between all of you. You know I'll do anything I can to help. Look at how wonderful you've been, making sure we have everything we need for Frankie since the moment we got here, especially now that she's not feeling well. Just tell me how to help and I'll keep trying." Jules felt like she'd just dug herself a hole she might not want to jump into, but how could she leave all these hurting people in the state they were in? There had to be a solution. She just needed to find it.

"You're already doing so much. I think if you can just stay around a little longer we'll turn a corner. I just need more time. A little more time," Tabitha opened her arms for a hug and Jules stepped right in. The smell of her elegant perfume and the feel of her expensive shirt against Jules's cheek brought her some comfort. Tabitha couldn't be the monster Michael kept painting her to be. He just needed to step back, put history behind him, and view his mother as the person she was today.

Jules grabbed her bag and headed for the waiting car out front. She thought for a moment she should head back in the house and let Michael know she was leaving. But he'd told her not to come back until she'd gotten a good break. She didn't want to send a text and have the whole room lighting up by the screen of his phone or waking either of them with the loud chirp of its speaker. Michael was exhausted. There was a good chance he'd put Frankie down in her crib and nodded off himself in the chair. She'd be back before he even knew she was gone.

That all made perfectly logical sense, but as the car pulled down the long driveway and away from the epically beautiful mansion, Jules felt as though she were

146

going to be sick. But the glow was back in Tabitha's eyes and that had to count for something.

Pulling up to the deserted parking lot of Forty-One Restaurant, Jules's hunger pangs were screaming. The smell as they stepped in the front door was like a wonderful assault on her senses. It made her think of the old cartoons where waves of smells came wafting off the food and lured the character off their feet and toward the source. She wasn't sure if she could just taste food in order to pick, she was feeling like she'd devour something.

"Chef Corbin takes this all very seriously. I don't want to insult him. This is a process, his process. When we step into his kitchen, he is the boss."

"Of course," Jules nodded, knowing she'd be willing to jump through a hoop of flames at this point if it meant she could taste whatever smelled so good.

"Ladies, thank you for joining me six minutes later than we agreed." The chef wore a tall white hat and a scowl as he folded his arms across his chest. His golden blond hair came out in tufts below the hat and his eyes were a glassy grey. "Now we'll only have four hours and fifty four minutes dedicated to this tasting. I have no idea what I'll shave off to make up for the time but we'll need to improvise."

"Five hours?" Jules whispered with a look of terror as she pleaded with Tabitha to tell her she'd heard him wrong.

"Did I not mention that?" Tabitha asked with a look on her face as though she were utterly forgetful.

Chapter Twenty-Four

"Michael, do you have a second?" Piper asked, looking as though she were moments away from facing a firing squad. Michael already had a terrible feeling and her expression pushed him over the edge.

"Did something happen to Jules? I expected her to come back and check on Frankie by now. It's been almost five hours. I had to leave her with Nicolette so I could take a bathroom break."

"No, nothing happened to Jules as far as I know. The doorman said she left with your mother a few hours ago to do something for the party but that's not what I need to talk to you about. Do you remember when you told me to do whatever I thought was needed to help the situation here. I believe your exact words were any means necessary."

"Yes," Michael said slowly, stretching the word out as though he were afraid to find out what Piper might have done.

"I may have panicked when Frankie was sick today, and I kind of did something that might have been over the top."

"What did you do?" he asked, holding his breath, but getting his answer a second later when a familiar voice echoed up the large hallway.

"How many damn rooms are there in this castle? I could get as lost as a blind dog in the woods in here."

"What did you do?" Michael asked again, now in an accusing tone. "You called Betty?"

"I did. I got nervous with everything going on, and I thought maybe she could help," Piper stuttered.

"Betty here, with my mother, in this place. You thought that would be a good thing? On what planet would that be a good thing?"

"In theory it sounded good," Piper said, nervously wringing her hands as Betty's voice grew closer. "But in reality I might be having some second thoughts."

"Here they are," Ben the doorman said as he guided Bobby and Betty around the corner to where Michael and Piper were standing.

"All things holy, Michael, where is Frankie? I get this call that she's sick and everything out here is a mess. Give me that baby." Betty looked as though she hadn't stopped moving since she got the call. She was still dressed in the clothes she would wear to the restaurant and her hair was pulled into a bun the way she wore it at work.

"She's in with the nanny right now," Michael explained feeling like his world was spinning off its axis.

"She doesn't need a nanny; she needs a doctor."

"We know; she's already seen a doctor. It's an ear infection. He ordered an antibiotic and we're going to start it tonight."

"Like hell," Betty shot back.

"Like hell what?"

"Antibiotics are a bunch of horse manure. They don't really work, and they usually do more damage than good. There are plenty of things that can be done for ear infections besides antibiotics. You can massage behind her ear to ease the pain. That should keep her from tugging on her ears. Some garlic can help too; it doesn't smell any worse than the ear does when it's infected. And she'll need lots of help getting to sleep. Some lavender drops in a bath should do the trick."

149

Bobby put his hand on Betty's shoulder and in a hushed voice tried to get her to calm down. "I know you're worried, but Michael and Jules know what they're doing."

"I don't think I'm going to rely on old wives' tales to treat my daughter. She doesn't have any of those symptoms. She's having no problem sleeping. As a matter of fact we've been having a hard time getting her to stay awake long enough to even take a bottle."

"What? That child doesn't sleep on a normal night. Ear infections are very painful. She shouldn't want to be lying down at all right now. She should be screaming like a banshee and wanting to be held," Betty pushed on, furrowing her brows.

"Well, she isn't," Michael explained with a shrug.

"Then that don't sound like any ear infection I've ever heard of. Who's the quack you've got treating her?"

"He's a renowned pediatrician who's been friends with my family for decades. His qualifications are extensive. He made a house call this afternoon and plans to come back in the morning." Michael's already frayed nerves were unraveling fast.

"Betty, why don't we give Michael and Bobby some time to talk while I take you to the kitchen for some tea," Piper offered as she touched Betty's elbow gently.

"I want to hold that baby. I need to see her for myself," Betty insisted as she shook off Piper's touch and stepped forward assertively.

"Mr. Cooper," Nicolette called from down the hallway. There was a frenzy in her voice that sent shivers down his spine.

"What is it?" he asked, hustling down the hallway with everyone following closely behind.

"There is blood in her ears. You need to call the doctor right away." Nicolette held up a burp cloth with a spot of pink blood in her shaking hand.

"I'll call him," Bobby said, and Michael tossed his phone back to him. Betty elbowed her way by him and practically stumbled into the nursery. She picked Frankie up out of the crib and flipped on the light. Frankie barely stirred as Betty looked her over and felt her head.

"She's not warm, no fever at all," she said kissing the crown of the baby's head.

"We just took her temperature a few minutes before you got here and it was still over one hundred one," Michael explained as he came in to get a closer look at Frankie's ears. Nicolette was right, they were leaking a pink bloody ooze that would have had Michael squirming in disgust in the days before he'd become a father. Now all it did was scare the shit out of him.

"The doctor is on his way. He'll be here in ten minutes. He said her eardrums likely burst and that it shouldn't be anything to rush her to the emergency room about but he'll take a closer look when he gets here," Bobby offered, clearly trying to stay calm.

"She's completely lethargic," Betty said, watching the flutter of Frankie's eyelids as the baby made a pathetic little sucking noise and then fell back into a slumber. "How long has she been this way?"

"Since just after breakfast this morning," Piper explained. "She didn't want much to eat and then after that just kept falling asleep and didn't want to wake up."

"It's nearly her usual bed time. Are you telling me she's been asleep all day, for almost twelve hours now?" Betty's concern made the hair on the back of Michael's neck stand up.

151

"Yes, but the doctor didn't seem too concerned about that," Michael told Betty defensively.

"When he gets here you may want to make sure he's not within swinging distance of my fists, because I'm not sure I'm going to be able to keep from slugging the fool." Betty was looking like steam might come pouring from her ears any second and Michael knew the threat of punching a doctor wasn't an exaggeration.

"Do you think we should take her to the hospital?" Michael asked, looking over at Piper and Bobby for them to weigh in too.

"I don't know anything about kids," Bobby shrugged. "If it were me I'd do whatever Betty thought."

"That should be everyone's philosophy on everything and this world would run much smoother," Betty shot back. "I'm not saying she needs to go to the emergency room. Those places are loaded with sick people and germs. I'm just not liking what I'm hearing about this doctor so far."

"I'm going to call Jules and see what she thinks," Michael said, gesturing to get his phone back from Bobby.

"She isn't here? Where the hell is she? Piper told me things were all screwed up out here but that sounds like an understatement so far." Betty was waving her arms around wildly.

"Jules went out with my mother. They're trying to get things ready for my sister's engagement party this weekend. It's convoluted. The best I can tell, my mother is trying to get Jules on her side so she can manipulate me into being her puppet and keeping the cash flowing around here. It's not going to happen though. Jules and I are leaving. We aren't even staying for the party. All of us are getting the hell out of here. I'll work remotely to get everything done here if I need to. This is getting out of control. We're all going home in the morning."

"I don't think that's possible," Dr. Sans interjected as he stepped into the nursery. "If the baby's eardrums have burst you won't be getting on a plane until she's feeling better."

"Then I'll rent a car and drive home," Michael retorted.

"I don't think you should put her through that stress. I would give her some time to rest up," Dr. Sans continued as he pulled out his otoscope and peered inside the baby's ears. Betty narrowed her eyes and looked like a coiled snake about to strike.

"Betty," Michael whispered with pleading eyes.

"This child is not well. She's acting completely out of sorts. I don't think it's just ear infections causing her problem."

"And who exactly are you?" Dr. Sans asked as he looked down his beak nose at Betty. "I'm guessing you aren't a doctor."

"It doesn't matter who I am. It matters who she is. And she is my entire world. I know every noise she makes. I know which toys she loves and which ones buzz too loud and make her cry. I cooked her first helping of sweet potatoes and know which songs she loves in the morning. You clearly don't know a damn thing about anything."

"Well you sound immensely qualified to diagnose this child since you know her favorite things," Dr. Sans scoffed arrogantly. A collective gasp escaped the lips of everyone in the room.

Betty seemed to brush over the doctor's comment and move on, which was not like her at all. "So you're saying my daughter is out planning a party while her child is sick? I'm asking for efficiency's sake. If I'm going to whoop this doctor's ass I'd like to know if my daughter is due for one too so I can get it all done at once."

Dr. Sans smirked and then let his face fall still as he read Betty's seriousness. He tucked his instruments away quickly and backed toward the door. "The child doesn't need to go to the emergency room. She'll be fine. Just let her rest." He nodded his head at Michael and then backed out of the room, clearly not wanting to leave himself vulnerable in the presence of what he likely thought was a crazy woman.

"She's just trying to help. Jules doesn't understand what's going on here with my mother, and she thinks she's helping." Michael felt like he needed to make a case for Jules and her choices, though realistically he was shocked to hear she'd left the house for so long.

"I don't care if she thinks she's liberating a war-torn country. The only thing she needs to be worrying about is this baby," Betty argued.

"Please don't come here and put more pressure on her. She's been overwhelmed with the baby for months and never said anything to me. The last thing she needs is you judging her choices right now. You set a very high standard, and she doesn't need that right now." Michael's lecture might have been misplaced, but his anger needed an outlet.

"First off, I didn't realize she was struggling," Betty said curtly. "Second, whatever the hell is going on out here with your mother amounts to a pile of beans.

Something isn't right with this baby. I might not be a doctor, but I know babies, and I especially know this baby."

"So then what do I do? Do we really go to the emergency room? I don't want to put her through all that," Michael croaked.

"No, we don't have to. She doesn't have a fever and she did eat some today, right? I'll watch her close tonight and if she's not acting differently in the morning then we'll go. But I'd like to talk to my daughter. Now."

"Ma?" Jules asked as she peeked her head into the nursery. "I just saw the doctor on the way out. He's talking to Michael's mother and saying some crazy southern woman threatened to give him a whooping. I should have known it was you."

"He's a moron. You need a second opinion, and you'll be getting one in the morning. Now, I don't want to leave this room until I understand what all the trouble is out here. I've heard drips and drabs but I want to know everything." Betty sat in the rocking chair with Frankie tucked in her arms and waited for a reply.

"I thought maybe we had an intruder or something, but I'm guessing I can call off the security now?" Tabitha asked as she looked around the room.

"Yes, Tabitha, I'm sorry. This is my mother," Jules said looking sheepish.

"Don't apologize for me. There ain't nothing sorry about me," Betty shot back as she continued to rock and barely spared Tabitha a glance.

"Oh, it's lovely to meet you. I didn't realize you were coming for a visit. We'd love to have you at the party this weekend." Tabitha's fake smile grew another inch wider, but Betty did not return the gesture. "Is there anything I can do to make your stay more comfortable?"

"You can leave," Betty stated flatly.

"Ma, stop it now," Jules shouted, taking a step between her mother and her mother-in-law.

Betty shrugged. "I'm not trying to be rude. I'm just wondering how everyone got all wonky the second they got out here. I'm not getting any calls or updates at all, then Piper calls me to tell me Frankie is sick, and I better come to help sort things out. So now I'm here, and I intend to do some sorting. I'd like some time alone with my kin to talk over what kind of mess is going on out here."

"I hardly think you'll be able to come in here and *sort out* any of this. It's quite presumptuous of you to think you could, actually. My family's complex problems aren't any of your concern." Tabitha arched an eyebrow at Betty and pursed her lips.

"When your family's complex problems start leaking like a rusty bucket all over my family then, yes, they becomes my concern. Now, this is your house, you don't have to leave. But if I tell all these people to pack their bags and leave with me right now they will. It ain't because I'm a bitch who orders them around, it's because they know I know what's good for them. So you can either step out of this room and let us talk or you can stay here and hope we don't mow you over on our way out."

Tabitha looked on in shock as Bobby, Piper, and Michael gave slight nods to indicate Betty was right. With that she huffed and turned on her heels to leave.

"Now someone shut that door," Betty ordered as she ran a finger over Frankie's smooth cheek.

"I can't believe you just did that, Ma. You have no idea what's going on here. You just assume that it's Tabitha causing the problems. What if you're wrong and you just insulted my mother-in-law?" Jules started with a raised voice and then lowered it to a hoarse whisper when Betty gestured toward the baby.

"You people don't cause problems. You walk in on a mess and try to fix it, but I don't know any of you to start trouble. Any woman who plans a party and drags the mother of a sick baby with her doesn't have my respect. I suppose she had a tactic for getting you to go with her today. I don't see you just leaving Frankie like that."

"No, she didn't have a tactic. She was upset and crying. Things are very tense here right now, and I was trying to help. I want her and Michael to have a relationship, and I'm hoping to be a part of bringing them together."

"Crying is a tactic. I'm not blaming you for going; I'm saying she had no business putting on some crocodile tears and asking you to leave your daughter for even a minute today. So if you want to fill me in on what's going on, I suggest you get to flapping your gums."

"Michael came out here on his own because he thought his baggage was too much for me to handle. He and his father had a very difficult relationship, and I think now that his dad is gone he's taking out his anger on his mother. I'm sure she hasn't been perfect, but he hasn't seen her in nearly a decade, and he's not even giving her a chance." Jules looked so confident in her response that it made Michael sad.

"Is that really what you think is going on here?" Michael asked, amazed at how out of sync he and his

157

wife were. "I told you my mother couldn't be trusted. She doesn't care about you, or any of us for that matter."

"Well, I've spent a good amount of time with her since we've gotten here, and she seems very much like a woman who's hurting. And you seem to be acting like someone who couldn't care less." Jules turned toward Betty to make her case. "He stood out on the lawn and told the media he was closing up everything she'd help to build, including charities she's dedicated years to."

"So?" Betty answered with a shrug. "I'm sure he's not just trying to be a mean old dog about it. Out with it, Michael; tell me why you're trying to shut everything down and get the hell out of here."

Michael scanned every face in the room. Bobby, Piper, Betty, and Jules were all standing there waiting to hear what it was that had him acting like he was on the warpath when, in fact, he was just defending what he'd worked so hard to finally find. "I always knew my mother and father were hungry for power. When I was younger I assumed it was a positive thing. It's part of what made me who I am. Some of my earliest memories are of me emulating my father. He made sure I had everything I ever wanted. Then after high school he set me on a course for a law degree. We started mingling in important circles and I met contacts that would fast track me on my way to a career. That summer I started working with him on a business level and I figured out what my job would actually be once I had my law degree. I got a peek behind the curtain of my father's world and I couldn't believe the things he did every day all in the name of wealth.

"His goal of me becoming a lawyer had nothing to do with his pride or his belief in me. He wanted me to protect him from all his crimes and hide all his lies. I was going to be the man he could trust. I'd be writing contracts for his mistresses to sign to make sure they didn't disclose the affair without harsh consequences. I'd be his guy to backdate paperwork to cover up inside trading. The laundry list of things a clever lawyer can do to cover up crimes is impressive."

"I wasn't trying to make an argument for your father. I never met him and I didn't have a chance to form an opinion about him," Jules explained as she cleared her throat, looking less comfortable by the second.

"When I realized this is what my father wanted out of me, my world caved in. He was my hero. I based my entire existence on becoming the man he was. I was devastated, and when I turned to my mother for sanity and comfort she told me to stop being ridiculous. She explained this was how the world worked and if I ever wanted to be successful I'd need to do what I was told."

"That's ugly," Betty said, shaking her head and mumbling some kind of prayer under her breath.

"And I asked her what would happen if I didn't. What if I wanted to go practice law somewhere else or even expose my father and his crimes? My answer was waiting for me the next morning. My house keys were gone. My credit cards were taken from my wallet and cut into confetti. My cell phone was smashed. The tires were taken off my car, and it was put up on blocks in the garage. The only thing I had to my name was the clothes on my back and a note from my mother. It read: *You have nothing without us.* I picked that up, stuffed it in my bag, and never looked back. I was dead set on proving to them I could be a success without them. I enlisted in the Marines and used the G.I. Bill to pay my way through school. And now, all these years later I have everything I've ever wanted in my life. I have family. Right here in this room I have people who would do, and have done, anything for me."

"That is awful, Michael, and I'm not making excuses for her actions. But that was a long time ago. Isn't there any chance she's changed?" Jules's chin was turned up as she kept trying to make her case.

"Oh honey, that's like finding bird shit in a cuckoo clock. Some people just ain't real and that ain't going to change over time. Any mother capable of not only expecting such things out of her son, but punishing him for not doing them is, excuse my language, a cold-hearted bitch. This here is your husband. You need to take his side and his hand and go home."

"That's very Christian of you, Mother," Jules responded sarcastically.

"Jules, it wasn't just that day. It's every moment leading up to that. I saw my mother destroy staff here for supposedly stealing her earrings. She publicly humiliated two of the housekeepers and made sure they couldn't work anywhere in this area again. Two days later the earrings turned up. They were in the pocket of a suit she'd dropped off at the dry cleaner. She never made that right. She meddled in every relationship I ever had and intentionally ended the ones she didn't like. My mother has an agenda for everything. These charities are a way to steal money and help her friends do the same. Her wanting us here right now has nothing to do with caring about us. She's looking for some last ditch effort to convince me to run my father's empire the same way he did so she can continue living the lifestyle she's accustomed to. Every conversation I've had with her so far has been either a threat or an attempt to blackmail me."

"Michael," Bobby interrupted, nervously clearing his throat as though he wasn't sure it was his place to say anything. "Why are you still here? Why bother getting involved? Couldn't you sign everything over to her and let her sink the ship on her own?"

"I would, but my sister's never known enough to get out. I guess my father learned his lesson with me. He didn't give her the chance to find out the kind of man he was. Instead, under the illusion of training her for the business world, he used her name to perpetuate dozens of crimes. Some are serious enough to land her in prison if they ever were to surface. By closing everything down I'm trying to bury that. But there are also a lot of people who benefit from my father's crimes. I'm trying to tactfully navigate that."

"Well if anyone can, it's you," Betty said with a warm smile. "That's your gift. You can tell someone to go screw themselves and make it so they thank you for the suggestion."

"Your sister didn't know what your father was doing?" Piper asked, clearly trying to sort out who knew what.

"No, I plan to tell her but not until everything is done. There isn't anything she can do at this point, and I don't want her to worry."

"Aren't you worried about getting in trouble for covering anything up?" Bobby asked.

"I'm not covering anything up really. I'm closing things down and hoping no one cares enough to come digging around. If my sister gets married and goes on to live a normal life, then no one is going to care about this stuff. It will just disappear. Or at least that's what I'm hoping."

"Isn't your mother the one who told you about your sister being in trouble? She obviously wanted you to help." Jules was starting to pace the room as she spoke.

"No, at first she just asked me to take over the business and protect my father's reputation by keeping everything that was locked up safe and sound. When that didn't work she played the card about my sister. She knew I wouldn't leave Josephine here to take the blame for something she didn't realize she was doing. It's not her fault. She shouldn't have had to think twice about trusting her own parents."

"Tabitha said she didn't know what was going on. She wouldn't have let him do that to Josephine." Jules was starting to sound more like she was trying to convince herself rather than anyone in the room. "You don't know for sure."

"I don't," Michael admitted. "But I'm not willing to risk you or Frankie on the off chance she's changed."

"What could she possibly do to us?" Jules asked through a breathy laugh that told Michael she really didn't understand.

"She can make it look like I'm having an affair so you leave me and take Frankie away. She could dig into any of our pasts and find one small linchpin that drives a stake right through our careers or our relationships. We've all made enough questionable choices over the last two years to provide her with some ammunition. She could spread a rumor, threaten us, or even plant evidence that makes us look like we committed a crime."

"You sound like you're on a television cop drama, Michael. You really believe your mother is capable of those things?" Jules scoffed.

"I don't believe it; I know it. She's done every single one of those things before. I've seen it with my own eyes."

Jules pursed her lips and drew in a deep breath. She seemed to be out of arguments in favor of his mother, or at least Michael hoped that was the case.

"How close are you to being done here?" Bobby asked, still looking uncomfortable.

"Lindsey is out right now chasing down a few more pieces of information about my father's associates. We're trying to understand his relationship with each of them to make sure I'm prepared to counter any threats they make. Best-case scenario: I meet with a few people tomorrow, file the dissolution forms with the secretary of state's office, and submit the funds remaining to the real beneficiaries of the charities. I got lucky; the way my father structured his will made it so I could make these moves without a vote from the board of directors for the charities. I'm in the home stretch."

"So wait, you're honestly planning on packing up and never looking back? You're willing to write your mother off?" Jules threw her hands up in exasperation.

"Jules, she wrote me off a long time ago. She's looking for a means to an end, and I refuse to be that for her. She's collected a fair amount of life insurance, and I'm structuring the manufacturing business in a way that it practically runs itself. It will turn a profit for her."

"I'm not worried about the money." Jules groaned, now sounding on the verge of tears.

"I know you're not, Jules, but that's the problem. That's *all* she's worried about." Michael moved toward her then stopped himself.

"Everyone in this room needs to be on the same page," Bobby said, looking directly at Jules. "That's how we've always gotten through this stuff before. Michael's goals need to be our goals. If he thinks the best thing to do is shut down anything he can and get back to Edenville, then that's what we should all be trying to do. I can help Lindsey out and Betty can stay with Frankie to give you a hand, Jules."

"I'm going to this party. I made a commitment to help, and I'm sticking with that. Is it really so crazy to hope this all works out? Look at everyone else's family. Bobby, you and your folks weren't getting along so well for years, but I saw you with them at your wedding. They were there to support you, and I know you're in a better place now with them than you've ever been. And Piper, I hopped in a car with you and ran off to New York City to find your biological father. Look at how well that turned out. You have people in your life now you can call family. Jedda and Willow have each other. Even Crystal is talking to her sister. Why can't I want that for Michael? If Michael has it, Frankie will too. My daughter deserves as many people in her life that love her as possible. You are all looking at me like I'm crazy to fight for that."

"Do I need to invest in some heavy duty Q-tips? Because your ears must be plumb full of wax if you didn't hear everything your husband just said about his mother. Does she really seem like somebody you want in your family?"

"But she *is* family. We all choose to be here, but she's Michael's mother. I just think that warrants a little extra hard work. I don't believe someone is just good or bad. I think things happen to people and they make choices. I look at my daughter and I can't imagine anyone would put anything, especially money, before their love for their child. I just don't want to believe that."

"Well, while you're busy not believing that, I think you're leaving yourself exposed. This woman sounds very manipulative. If Michael doesn't trust her then I don't trust her. And while I think your motives are admirable, you're being foolish." Betty was still rocking rhythmically and in between doling out her opinions she was humming sweet songs to Frankie.

"Look at this room, Ma. She found out about us at about ten o'clock at night and by lunchtime the next day she'd already had all of this done. All for Frankie."

"Of course, because Frankie has such expensive taste. Just the other day I heard her complaining about how the dust ruffle on the crib at my house was peasant-like and she wouldn't stand for it." Betty rolled her eyes. "Nothing in this room is for Frankie. The child bites her own toes and thinks spit bubbles are magical. This room was about impressing you."

"Frankie could have the best of everything if we made room in our lives for Michael's family. I'm not saying I want to move from Edenville; I'm just wondering what advantages she could have if we kept the door open here. Great schools, prestigious clubs, it's endless what she could accomplish. But Michael hasn't even considered that as an option. "

"It's not too often I don't respond to something. But that's so asinine that I won't even engage you on that. You're wearing your rear end as a hat right now, that's all

I'll say about that." Betty looked like she was literally biting her tongue.

"I'm still going to the party. I hope all of you come too. Josephine is Michael's sister, and it doesn't sound like she has a history of being some kind of monster." The tone Jules was using told Michael she didn't believe his mother to be as bad as he was saying. "She's Frankie's aunt, and I've committed to being there to celebrate. If you still want to leave the moment the party is over then I'll go. As long as Frankie is healthy enough to travel."

"I'm going to be here with this baby all night and in the morning. If she's not back to her old self, we'll take her to the hospital. This party is in two days, right?"

"Yes," Michael said as he exhaled and rolled his eyes knowingly. Betty's raised eyebrows and stern look told him she was about to propose a compromise.

"Then let's just be hospitable guests until the party is over. Then we all agree to leave. I don't care if we have to drive back one hour at a time to accommodate Frankie. Let's agree that Edenville is the best place for all of us, and then y'all can talk through how to move forward. But at least you'll be surrounded by people you can trust."

"Fine." Michael and Jules spoke the word in unison and then stared down at their shoes like disappointed children.

"Now tell me, I'm feeling a bit peckish. Where's the kitchen? I'd like to make myself a sandwich before I settle in to watch Frankie for the night."

"It's not that kind of kitchen, Ma," Jules explained. "You can't just walk in there and make yourself something to eat. They have a staff. You tell them what you'd like, and they make it for you. They'll even bring it in here with everything you need." The smile on Jules's face faded quickly as she seemed to realize Betty was neither impressed nor excited about this.

"That sounds an awful lot like what it used to be like in the South when I was a kid. Since then folks have worked damn hard to make sure no one was in the business of ordering anyone around like a servant. I'm plenty capable of making my own sandwich. Just point me in that direction. I don't need to be waited on."

"It's not like that, Ma. They get paid a fair wage. It's a job just like any other."

"I don't know about that actually," Piper said, twisting her face up slightly. "I don't know if there's a paycheck in the world big enough for them to put up with the way they are treated here. Maybe you haven't seen it yet, but I have. It's kind of twisted."

"I guess I've been blind to everything lately." Jules's anger was starting to bubble over. "I'll have them make you a sandwich, and I'll bring it here for you. I'll be sure to ask them very nicely. Heaven help us if we ever have a falling out like this. I didn't realize all of you would give up so easily. Whatever happened to fighting for family?"

Jules was out the door, her shoes slapping hard against the marble floor. The room was silent for a moment and then, like usual, Betty sliced the quiet open with sharp words of wisdom. "I think that woman has done a number on my child. I don't know what kind of bull she's been feeding her, but it certainly sounds like Jules is falling for it. All I know is, I trust you, Michael."

"I think that's part of the problem. When I bailed on Jules it put a little fracture in her trust for me. When she found out I'd been hiding all of this from her the crack got a little bigger. My mother is great at finding those cracks and turning them into canyons. A lot of this is my fault. I should have just told Jules from the beginning about my family. If I had she'd be in here right now helping us get the hell out of here." Michael ran his hands through his hair feeling completely exhausted.

"I can't disagree with you there. It'll be a fine day when all of you finally start just telling each other everything right out of the gate. Half our heartaches wouldn't exist if you did. Now go on and get done whatever you need to. I'm going to get this baby eating and hopefully ready to leave Sunday morning when that party is all done and behind us."

"I'm really glad you're here, Betty," Michael admitted with a warm smile.

"Just think of me like a bad penny, always turning up."

"Thank goodness for that," Piper said, and she, Bobby and Michael crept out of the nursery.

Chapter Twenty-Five

"She's looking more like herself this morning," Betty said as she rubbed her tired eyes. Jules had told her a hundred times she didn't need to spend the entire night in the nursery, but her mother would not be swayed. She sat vigil by Frankie's crib, dozing lightly in the rocking chair and checking on her temperature often. "She hasn't been warm all night. I haven't felt a fever since I got here."

"She does look more alert this morning. Maybe her ears are doing better. Thanks for watching her last night. I felt better knowing you were here." Jules still felt a prickly frustration with everyone's pessimistic attitude, but there was no denying having her mother around brought her some comfort that she couldn't get anywhere else in the world. But wasn't that the problem?

"It's just you and me here, girl. You want to talk to me more about what's going on with you? I know there has to be more to this than just you thinking Michael's mother can be better than she is."

"I think something might be wrong with me," Jules blurted out, biting at her lip to try to combat the tears, but they came anyway. There was something about having her mother within arm's reach that made it impossible not to open up.

"There isn't a damn thing wrong with you, sweet child. You're my daughter. I made you. You're perfect. Me and God, we don't make mistakes." Betty placed Frankie back in her crib for a moment and pulled her daughter in for a hug.

"I'm really sad all the time, Ma. Like really sad. I'm crying most nights, just sitting alone wondering what's wrong with me. I'm screwing all of this up. I thought by now I'd feel better, that I'd be a better mother, but I'm not. I'm failing her and Michael. I can't even get the dishes done some days. I can't even nurse her. I have to pump and give her a bottle because I couldn't even do that right. I forget everything, and Frankie has no routine. I can't get her down at the same time every night. I read all these articles and by her age I should be doing all these things with her. I should be teaching her all these things and I'm not. I don't know how." Jules was in a full out sob as she tried to string her words together. Anyone other than Betty likely would have stopped her by now, complaining they couldn't understand her, but her mother spoke this language fluently. She'd been learning it her entire life, raising Jules. "What if she turns out all wrong? What if Michael can't deal with the house being a mess or that I can't make dinner? That's why I thought he left, you know. I thought he finally figured he could do better than what I was giving him. I've barely been a wife lately, and I'm struggling to keep my head above water as a mom. Those are my only two jobs and I'm not doing either of them well."

"I wish you'd have said something to me," Bettys said, wiping away a tear of her own.

"How could I? How do you tell the best mother in the world that you can't handle being one yourself? Every single night growing up you had dinner on the table. You and Dad spent so much time just being in love. You got everything done. You were perfect. You're still perfect. Look at all the people you mother. How do I face you and tell you I'm not sure what I'm doing?"

"Your memories are from when you were in school, not as a baby. You don't remember the nights I spent begging for some kind of break. We ordered so much pizza the first year after you were born they knew our order by heart. Do you know you fell off my bed? You rolled right onto the floor and landed with a thump I can still hear right now; it's etched into my brain and will be there forever. And nursing? You were on formula for the same reason. You and I just couldn't figure it out together, and I figured it was better you eat rather than us keep driving each other nuts for something that wasn't happening. I made so many mistakes with you. There are still days I can't believe you survived my failures and came out so wonderful."

"I didn't know that. I just assumed you always had everything figured out the way you do now."

"I don't have everything figured out now. I still make plenty of mistakes. Like the way I told Clay not to come out here because you aren't his daughter. I didn't mean it the way I said it, but I also didn't take it back either. I know I hurt him, but I left it there between us. Your old mama still makes plenty of mistakes. I do my share of crying over them too. I'm sorry if I didn't make it clear you could come to me with this. I'm always here for you. You haven't done anything wrong." Betty smoothed down Jules's hair and hugged her so tight she felt her loose pieces fitting back together, even if for only a moment.

"I think that's why I'm pushing so hard for Michael to forgive his mother. I don't want to believe anyone can truly act that way toward her child. I need to believe there is hope for them because I'm afraid one day Frankie is going to feel the same way about me and she might not forgive me for my failures."

171

"I think that's why God makes babies forget. You can't be expected to get all this right on the first try. No one tells you how hard it's going to be and how different you feel from what you thought you would. But it does sound like you've got more than just the baby blues. I think you need to talk to someone."

"I don't want people to know I'm not doing a good job. If they think I'm not happy being a mom then they'll look at me differently."

"With any other group of people I might agree with you. I'm not sure you know it yet, but this little bunch here isn't average. They won't judge you. They'll help you. We can call Josh when we get back to Edenville. He loves you, and he'll know where to start." Betty looked down at Frankie who'd rolled herself into a sitting position and was smiling up at them. "She is definitely feeling better."

"Thank goodness," Jules said as she scooped her daughter up and kissed her neck in the way that always produced a giggle.

"Mrs. Cooper," Nicolette interrupted with a little knock on the doorframe. "I thought the baby might be hungry. I warmed some of your milk for her."

"Thank you, Nicolette. She seems so much better this morning. Almost back to her old self." Jules forced a smile and hoped Nicolette could ignore her wet eyes.

Nicolette nodded, handed over the bottle, and backed out of the room silently and obediently.

"I'll give her the bottle. You go ahead and get a hot shower, and I'll meet you for breakfast." Betty took Frankie back and settled into the rocking chair.

"Are you sure you want to eat breakfast with everyone? I know you don't like Michael's mother but I don't want to make things any worse then they are."

"Believe it or not I am very good at biting my tongue. Just because I don't normally choose to do it doesn't mean I don't know how."

"Thank you, Ma," Jules croaked as the tears came again. "For everything. I don't know what I'd do without you."

"God's too smart to let us find out."

Chapter Twenty-Six

"What a lovely dining room," Betty said with a smile, and Jules felt a small ripple of relief flow over her. Her mother was trying. That meant something to her. It wasn't easy for Betty to keep her true opinions to herself.

"Thank you, it's due for a renovation again. I like to keep things fresh and have it redesigned every couple years." Tabitha took the napkin from her glistening porcelain plate and placed it across her lap. "Now, I've had the cook put together a lovely breakfast this morning. I'm so glad to see little Frankie feeling better."

"She just took a whole bottle," Betty explained as Piper, Bobby, and Lindsey entered the dining room and took their seats around the long table. The staff was buzzing around and Jules could see her mother's eyes following them around the room.

As a young woman with her hair pulled into a bun and pinned in place offered Betty her choice of drinks, Jules could sense something was about to happen. "I'll just have water, dear," Betty replied as she warmly touched the woman's mocha-colored arm. "Tell me, where are you from? I love your accent. It's beautiful."

"Thank you. I'm from the Dominican Republic, Miss," the woman answered obediently as she tried to quickly step away, but Betty caught her arm gently.

"I've always wanted to go there. I hear it has the most amazing blue water. What's your favorite thing about it there?" Betty's look of sincere interest had the woman warming for a moment, until her eyes darted up and met Tabitha's.

"It's hard to miss anything when I live in a wonderful place such as this."

"But the food, there must be food you don't have the chance to eat up here. I'd love to travel the world and try food from every nation. What would I have if I went to the Dominican Republic?"

Unable to deflect the question or hold back her excitement to answer it, the young woman lit with a smile. "My mother makes the best smoked herring. I still dream about them sometimes at night and wake up hungry. Her secret was leeks."

"I'll have to have you scratch down that recipe if you'd consider sharing it. I own a restaurant, and I'm always searching for new items for the menu. What's your name, dear? Maybe we'll name it after you."

"I'm Gloria, and I'd be happy to write that down for you. It would be an honor for you to serve it in your restaurant."

Betty extended her hand and Gloria looked as though she wasn't sure why. "I'm Betty. It's a pleasure to meet you. If you have time after breakfast I'd like to hear more about where you are from."

"That might be difficult since she'll be scraping food off dishes and then going to make up the bedrooms," Tabitha interjected.

"Yes, of course, ma'am," Gloria said as she scurried away.

"We try not to treat the staff that way. It sets a poor precedence." Tabitha tapped her mug and gestured for more coffee.

"I'm sorry about that," Betty countered. "I do have a nasty habit of treating people like human beings. I'm trying to cut that out."

"That's likely because you've never had to manage a staff before. If you start talking to them that way they'll walk all over you. Before you know it they're asking for time off to visit that country you talk to them about, or they're stealing right under your nose."

"You don't have to tell me," Betty said, nodding in agreement. "You know what they say, kindness breeds evil."

"Who says that?" Bobby asked, and Jules cursed him for being oblivious to the obvious sarcasm and making this moment last any longer than necessary.

"A moron," Betty replied curtly as she backed her chair away from the table. "I suddenly don't feel very hungry. I think I'll take a walk."

"Ma, please," Jules begged as she took the plate of tiny pieces of toast and lay them out in front of Frankie.

"Jules," Piper suggested, with a look like she was scrambling to change the subject, "I bet your mother hasn't seen the fountain out back. I'll walk with her."

A moment later they were out the door and the dining room was absent of any chatter. The only noises were the clanking of forks and clearing of throats.

Finally Bobby broke the awkwardness, unfortunately with a question that only made it worse. "Where is Michael?"

"He's working," Jules answered flatly. The real answer was that he was scanning all the documents to officially file them.

The dining room door swung open as Spencer, the gala's concierge, walked in. "Mrs. Cooper, this just arrived for you. I think you should open it right away."

Tabitha shot to her feet. "And is Josephine here yet?"

"She's just pulled in," Spencer said with a wicked smile.

"What perfect timing. Have her meet me in her father's office. I need to see her immediately."

"What's going on?" Jules asked, feeling a vice tighten around her heart. "Is it about the party?"

"It's family business," Tabitha said coolly as she stepped out of the dining room and left them all looking around in confusion.

"What do you think that was about?" Lindsey asked, leaning nearer to Bobby.

"I'm guessing some last ditch effort to keep Michael here doing what she wants him to do."

"Should I be worried?" Jules asked, biting at her lip nervously.

"Yes," Lindsey shot back until Bobby gave her a sideways look. "But I'm sure it'll be fine.

"That's not very convincing," Jules said as she pushed away the plate of food that had been laid before her.

"You don't have anything to worry about, Jules. Michael has this all under control and we're all here together. We're not going to let anything happen. You know how we are in these situations."

"I'm starting to think Tabitha is an entirely different situation than anything we've dealt with before." Jules ran a hand over her daughter's wispy hair and down her cheek.

"And I'm guessing we're entirely different than anything she's ever dealt with before. It'll be fine."

Chapter Twenty-Seven

"Mother, I don't really have time for you to sit in here and stare at me. I'm in the middle of something." Michael wished the look in his mother's eye wasn't getting to him, but it was. She looked downright victorious and that wasn't something she would fake.

"We're just waiting for your sister. She needs to hear this too. And don't worry if it keeps you from sending those papers. After this you won't need to." Tabitha patted the large envelope on her lap and smiled.

"What is this about?" Josephine asked as she stepped into the office and read the tension stewing there.

"This is about Michael stopping this nonsense about dismantling our fortune and our future. This ends today."

"Mother, I think we've covered this pretty extensively. I'm not staying here. Dad left everything to me, and I'm not continuing the mess he made. Now if you'll both excuse me I need to get these documents scanned and emailed."

"Well then you better give your sister a kiss because this might be the last time you aren't separated by bars." Tabitha split open the envelope and pulled out a small stack of paperwork.

"Mother?" Josephine asked as the blood drained from her face. "What are you talking about?"

"You killed your father. The proof is right here. I've been waiting for the report, trying like hell to stall your brother, and now it's finally here." The joy on her face was scary.

"He died of a heart attack," Michael scoffed.

"No, he died from head trauma. The heart attack wasn't the cause of death. He had quite the hit to the side of the head."

"So he hit his head on the desk after falling over from the heart attack. What does that have to do with Jo?" Michael was trying to keep his face stern but his nerves were raging.

"Everything," Josephine whispered as her legs shook and she braced herself against the wall.

"What are you talking about?" Michael asked, his anxiety welling up to a level he thought he might drown in.

"I found out, Michael. I knew what he was trying to do to me. I was going to be his scapegoat. He set me up, and I could have gone to jail for the things he had me do. I was furious."

"You knew what he had done? Why didn't you tell me that? You were walking around talking about Dad like he was still your hero." Michael ran his hands through his hair with exasperation.

"Mother told me it would be better if I didn't tell you what had happened. She said it had been so long since we'd seen you we didn't know if you would just turn me in. She promised me she'd handle everything."

"Oh I'm handling it," Tabitha smirked.

"Tell me what happened, Jo," Michael begged.

"I found out he was using me to essentially rob people and steal from the government. There was inside trading and all sorts of things with my name all over them. I came in here and confronted him. I grabbed the first thing I saw and hurled it at him. It was that trophy he had from the polo match he won in college. It was so heavy, and it hit him right in the head. He fell out of his

179

chair and on to the floor. I screamed for help. By the time the ambulance came Mother had already picked up the trophy and hid it. They just assumed he'd had a heart attack because of his history and hit his head on the way down. But he didn't. I killed him."

"Where is the trophy now?" Michael asked, thinking exclusively as a lawyer for a moment.

"I have it," Tabitha explained looking very proud of herself. "It's somewhere very safe just waiting for the moment to turn it over to the police if that becomes necessary. It won't be hard for them to match it up to your father's injuries," she turned her gaze on Josephine, "or find your fingerprints on it."

Josephine's face crumpled. "Why are you doing this? You planned this from the beginning? I thought you were trying to protect me, but you were being strategic? For God's sake, I'm your daughter."

"Exactly. You are my daughter and by now you should know better. At least your brother realized early on that I would do anything to keep this family at our present status. I'm not going to start buying dresses off the rack and clipping coupons. I gave your father almost four decades of my life so when I was finally rid of him I could live the life I've always wanted. I'm not letting your brother's conscience get in my way."

"What do you want?" Michael asked, knowing he couldn't negotiate if he didn't know her specific terms.

"You stay here. You recant what you said to the media and let them know we've reconsidered and intend to keep everything business as usual. If you do, then I won't expose what your sister did."

"That's it? That's all it will take?" Josephine asked, looking desperately at Michael. "Just do what she wants, and this can all go away."

"Do what she wants? That means walking away from my home and dragging my family into this toxic hellhole. It means compromising myself to the point that I will eventually get caught and end up in jail myself. None of this is sustainable. The fact that Dad never got caught was miraculous. That luck is going to run out. He knew that; it's why he started shifting things into your name, Jo. I can't do this."

"So you are going to just let her send me to jail? I can't go to jail for murder, Michael. You have to understand, I was heartbroken he would betray me. I loved him. He was my hero. I didn't mean to do it."

"I know that and a jury would too. There was nothing premeditated about it. It was an accident. You didn't mean to kill him."

"A jury?" Josephine asked as she began to sob. "You can't honestly be considering letting her turn me in? I'm about to start my life and be married. I can't go to prison. Please, you're my brother. You have to protect me."

Michael looked from his mother to his sister and wondered how he'd ended up tied to these people. What miserable things had he done in a past life to be born into this family? "I need time to think about it, Jo. I can't make that promise right now. I have my family to worry about."

"I'm your family," she cried. "I'm your baby sister and I need you."

"Michael," Jules shouted as she rounded the corner of the office and plowed her way in. "It's Frankie. She

Danielle Stewart

just threw up, and she's lethargic again. We're taking her to the emergency room right now."

Michael shot up from his chair and grabbed his wife's hand as they rushed together toward the front of the house. Everything that was crushing him fell away, and a new boulder of worry took its place.

Chapter Twenty-Eight

As Jules strapped Frankie into her car seat in the back of the chauffeured car Michael looked around frantically for Bobby. He needed his best friend's help, and as though a super hero signal had been sent up to the sky, Bobby appeared.

"I need your help, man," Michael said, as Bobby and Lindsey approached quickly.

"Is she all right? I saw her get sick at the table; that was so scary." Bobby peeked over Michael's shoulder and tried to get a look at Frankie.

"Jules, I need you and your mom to go on ahead of me. I'll be right behind you. I need to talk to Bobby."

"Is everything okay?" Jules asked, and her tired face was drawn down with fear.

"It will be. I won't be more than ten minutes behind you, I promise. Just get our baby to the hospital, and I'll be right there." He leaned into the car and planted a kiss on his daughter and his wife before shutting the door and tapping the roof firmly to indicate to the driver to go.

As the car pulled off down the long driveway, Piper jogged up and the four of them stood there for a moment watching the car disappear.

"What's going on?" Piper asked looking panicked. "Why didn't you go with them?"

"I have a problem. I need to talk to you, Bobby. Can you ride with me?" Michael asked, flagging another car to pull up.

"Can't we help too?" Lindsey looked insulted.

"You've been really helpful already. The information you gathered on my father's associates was perfect. But this is something different entirely. I don't want to get

Danielle Stewart

you involved in it if I don't have to. It's not fair to you. Once I tell you, you'd have an obligation to act, and I don't want to put you in that position." Michael looked down at his watch and reached for the car door.

"You don't know me that well," Lindsey said shrugging. "You forget, I was the one in the cabin with Bobby the day Christian killed the man hunting Piper. I'm the one who convinced Bobby to cover it up. I look at the big picture, the greater good. You can trust me."

Michael glanced up at Bobby quickly and read his barely perceptible nod of agreement.

"Fine. This is very time sensitive. My mother is blackmailing my sister, and I need to find something to protect her. I can't give in to the terms my mother is demanding. I need other options, and I need you to find me something." Michael rubbed at the tension that had built in his temple.

"What could she possibly have on your sister?" Piper asked, looking skeptical.

"This isn't easy for me to say." Michael drew in a deep breath and reminded himself that there was no other solution but to ask for help, even if he hated doing that. "My sister knew my father was setting her up. I didn't think she was aware of it but she was. On the day my father died she argued with him about it. In the heat of the moment she picked up a trophy he kept in his office and threw it at him. The base is solid marble and it hit him in the head. My mother has a report from the medical examiner saying the cause of death was that blow to the head."

"She killed him?" Piper asked, catching her breath at the realization.

184

"No," Michael barked back, cutting through the air with his hand. "No, she didn't mean to do it. I need you to dig into this and find me something I can use to counter my mother."

Bobby ran his hand over his nearly shaved head and gave the situation some thought. "What does your mother want from you?"

"She wants me to tear up the papers I was about to send off and stay here to run the circus. I can't do that." Michael shook his head adamantly.

"You can't move forward with your original plan. You're not going to send your sister to jail." Piper's voice was stern as she raised her hands to her hips. "That's not what we do. We help the people who deserve it."

"I wouldn't be sending her to jail. She made a choice that day. Don't you think I wanted to throw a hundred things at my father over the years? But I didn't. She lost control. Plus it's not as though this was premeditated. She certainly didn't plan it. With a sympathetic jury and one hell of a lawyer she could walk away with a limited punishment."

"Or?" Lindsey asked, seeming to already know the answer to that question.

"Or she could be convicted and spend the rest of her life in jail."

"You need to help her, Michael." Piper stared straight up at him with a fierce look in her eye.

"I'd be trading my life for hers because of something she chose to do. It would only be a matter of time before I'd get caught up in my father's mess and arrested or sought out by someone he double-crossed. I can't be under my mother's thumb for years to come just because she's holding this over our heads. I don't know what I'm supposed to do here. It's why I need some other option. Get me something. Find me a bargaining chip and do it quickly. I need to get to the hospital. Please just get me something."

"I'll ride with you," Piper offered, but Michael waved her off.

"Stay with my sister please. Just keep an eye on her and try to keep her calm. She's just been hit with harsh reality. I don't want her flying off the handle. You guys know I hate asking for help, but I do appreciate it."

"Just call us when you know anything about Frankie. Above anything else, that's what I care about." Bobby extended his hand and shook Michael's firmly then they leaned in for a quick thump of their chests before they let go of each other's hands.

"Be careful. Try to stay out of trouble," Michael called through the half-opened car window as the vehicle started to speed off. "Don't be yourselves," he added with a shout across the large driveway. He leaned forward and tapped the driver on the shoulder. "I want to be to the hospital in the next ten minutes. I don't care how you have to drive to make that happen. Just get me there."

Chapter Twenty-Nine

"What if something is really wrong, Ma. I don't know what I'll do if Frankie is really sick." Jules was lying in the hospital bed with her daughter curled against her as the doctor walked in with Michael two steps behind him. Even though she had Betty by her side, these new arrivals felt like the cavalry arriving.

"Mrs. Cooper, I hear your daughter is not feeling well. I'm Dr. Dracon, the head of pediatrics for the hospital, and we're going to get to the bottom of this. Tell me about her symptoms." Without hesitation the doctor began examining Frankie as she lay sleeping on the bed. It was frightening to see how sound her sleep was and how she could be moved without stirring.

"Yesterday morning after breakfast she started acting strangely and wouldn't eat. Then she fell asleep, which she never does that time of day. She slept most of the day away and was hard to wake. The nanny took her temperature multiple times and she had a fever over one hundred one. We called the pediatrician and he came by and told us her ears were very infected. He prescribed some antibiotics that we were going to get that night. Sometime that evening her eardrums burst and she had bloody gunk in both ears. She continued to be really lethargic and not acting at all like herself."

"Her eardrums have not burst. Her ears are pristine actually. No infection to speak of. Are you sure that's what the pediatrician said? Who does she see?"

"We're here from out of town. My husband's family knows a pediatrician, Dr. Sans, and he made a house call. I'm positive that is what he told us."

"Did you start the antibiotics?"

"No," Betty cut in. "I don't think they are necessary for ear infections, especially in someone so young. I had a cousin who suffered as a child and he did fine with some home remedies. I talked them out of using them. Plus, hardly any of the baby's symptoms seemed like those of an ear infection to me."

"I'd have to agree with you on both counts. I don't like to give antibiotics at such a young age. The body can often fight the infection, and they clear up on their own. I just like to manage the child's pain, but ear infections don't seem to be Frankie's problem. I'll reach out to Dr. Sans and get some more information, but at this point, looking at Frankie's ears I don't see any indication of current or recent ear infection. So let's try to get to the bottom of this. She's lethargic, has she been consistently that way since yesterday?"

"She was spry as a spring chicken this morning when she woke up, and she took a full bottle of breast milk. I thought for sure she was on the mend." Betty looked over solemnly at a snoring Frankie.

"How long after the bottle did she get sick and begin acting lethargic again?" Dr. Dracon asked, scratching some notes down on the chart.

"Maybe twenty minutes later," Betty offered, looking at Jules for confirmation. When Jules nodded, the doctor made another note.

"Mrs. Cooper, is there a chance you are passing anything to her through your breast milk? Have you been drinking or taking any medication that might be impacting her?"

"What? No, of course I haven't. I'm very careful about what I put in my body. I don't drink, and I'm not on any medications." Jules felt her palms become sweaty and her heart start racing as she considered she could be making the baby sick by accident.

"I'm sorry, I just needed to ask. Sometimes mothers do it without realizing the impact it might be having. This could be something as simple as an allergy. You may be eating something that doesn't agree with her, or she may be eating something new that doesn't sit well."

"It would cause this type of drowsiness?" Michael asked, furrowing his brows in concern.

"Not usually, but there are some cases where it happens. Everyone reacts to allergens differently. We'll run a series of tests as well. The nurse will be in momentarily to start an IV and draw some blood."

"No," Jules said feeling the tears starting. "She's too little for that. She can't have that sticking out of her arm and hurting her."

"Unfortunately we need it. If the situation turned emergent we'd need quick access for delivering life saving medicines. I promise our pediatric nurses are wonderful at this. They know exactly how to care for someone your daughter's age. We're going to get to the bottom of this. I'm going to go give Dr. Sans a call to see where the confusion came in about the ear infection, and then we'll be taking your daughter up for some more tests."

"I want to be with her," Jules insisted. "Every second. Every test. I want to be with her."

"I understand Mrs. Cooper, however there are some places in the hospital—" The doctor was silenced by a wave of Jules's hand.

"I don't care. I want to be with her."

"All right. We'll make sure." Dr. Dracon stepped out of the small room and Jules went back to affectionately stroking her daughter's cheek.

"What is going on, Michael? What is wrong with her?" Jules pleaded, hoping he had an answer.

"I don't know," he admitted as he came up behind her and rested his large warm hand on her back. "But we aren't leaving here until we find out and know what to do."

"Something's going on though, with your mother? She's done something you need to deal with? You can't be in both places," Jules sniffled.

"I don't need to be. That's what our best friends are for. They're taking care of it now. You don't have to worry, Jules. I'm not going anywhere."

Chapter Thirty

The sun was setting on this horrific day, and Michael had no more answers than when the hot yellow globe had risen that morning.

"I've tried to reach the doctor who made the house call a few times but can't locate him. He doesn't seem to be practicing medicine at any particular place anymore. But even without speaking to him I've completely ruled out any ear trouble at all. Her eardrums are intact and there is really no sign of recent infection. Her urine looks good, and the fluids she's been given have perked her up quite a bit. There is a chance she was dehydrated, but we can't say for certain that was the case. We'd like to admit her overnight while we wait for the rest of her blood work results. Her counts seem fine, but we're looking for any kind of toxins and that takes a little longer. I think keeping her here on steady fluids is the right thing to do for this evening."

"Thank you, doctor," Michael said, extending his hand and shaking the doctor's firmly.

"So we still don't know?" Jules asked as she paced around the room. Frankie had been moved upstairs and was now sitting up in the hospital's steel cage crib. "She looks like she's in prison, and we still don't know any more about why she's been sick."

"She does look better though," Betty offered as she leaned over the side of the crib and dangled a toy for Frankie to grab, which she happily did.

"Have you heard from Bobby? Has he made any progress in helping your sister?" Jules bit nervously at her nails as she continued to pace the room. This full disclosure thing was new for Michael. Normally he'd have tried to handle his sister's situation much more quietly. The lawyer in him wanted to make sure his wife had some plausible deniability should she ever be asked about the situation. But he knew if he wanted to start rebuilding complete trust with his wife, something she deserved was the constant truth. And Betty, well she was just there and the right kind of nosy to find anything out anyway, so he'd told her too.

"I called and left them voicemails earlier in the day, letting them know how Frankie was doing, but I haven't heard back. It's getting late; I'm sure they'll be checking in soon." Michael glanced down at his watch and did the math in his head. His mother had given him twenty-four hours to make his decision, and he had about twelve of those left. His sister had called a couple times throughout the day to check on Frankie and melt sadly on the other end of the phone about her situation and the fear it was causing. He just had to put his faith in his friends.

A quiet knock on the door had them all turning quickly, expecting to see the doctor with some results. Instead it was Bobby peering in the room cautiously and then perking up when he saw Frankie looking alert and with more color in her cheeks.

"Sorry to barge in, guys, but I need Michael." Bobby waved at Jules who gave a small wave back but then went straight back to biting her nails.

"I can't leave, Bobby. I want to stay here with Frankie. Can we just step out into the hallway and talk?"

"We have somewhat of a situation. It's time sensitive. I just want to get your opinion before we move forward," Bobby explained.

"Out with it," Betty called, narrowing her eyes at Bobby. "We already know the whole story. No need to step into the hallway. I want answers too."

"This might be something that would be better if you didn't know about it. Less chance you'll get in trouble," Bobby pressed.

"Out with it," Betty repeated loudly and gestured for him to start talking.

Bobby looked over at Michael who nodded that it would be fine to disclose anything in front of them. "Suit yourself. Lindsey and I found a money trail between your mother and the medical examiner. It's complicated, though, because there was a pass through. She used Dr. Sans to funnel the money to the medical examiner. Fifty thousand dollars over the last week. She has it marked as payment for the home visits over the last couple of days, but it doesn't make any sense. The dates don't even match up. It's a cover-up and a lousy one."

"What do the two doctors have to do with each other at all?" Michael asked, shaking his head in confusion.

"We didn't know, which is why we went to pay a visit to Sans but he panicked, clearly hiding something, and tried to run."

"Did you catch him?" Jules asked, dropping her hands to her side? "Our doctor wants to talk to him."

"Lindsey's knee must be pretty well healed because she chased his ass down and leveled him in a hurry. The problem was the information we came across was not obtained legally with a warrant. We are outside our jurisdiction so we couldn't arrest the guy."

"What do we do now?" Michael asked, the wheels spinning in his head as he tried to think of a legal plan.

"That's why I'm here. I had to make a judgment call. He struck me as a runner, and the kind of guy who might disappear and have the means to stay that way. I restrained him. As a matter of fact he's still restrained. Now I just need to know what you want me to do with him."

"You kidnapped him?" Michael asked incredulously, slapping his hand to his forehead.

"You need to get him to talk," Betty said flatly, cutting through everyone's nerves in the room. "If he's the go-between then he knows both of them. He struck me as a coward. I'd bet with some pressure you could get him to spill the beans and cooperate."

"I can't interrogate him under these conditions and expect anything to hold up in court. I'm a cop. I know better."

"I ain't," Betty said with a shrug. "I'd be happy to find a way to get him to tell the truth. Then he can tell that same truth to the cops here."

"You aren't trained in interrogation, Betty. This isn't some kid who shoplifted a candy bar. He's not going to just tell you what you want to hear because you ask him nicely."

"Nice has nothing to do with what I was thinking about." Betty laughed.

"No," Michael cut in. "We need to handle this through legal channels. He's not dumb. He'll want immunity, and we need to find a way to get it for him if we want him to talk."

"You're a lawyer, Michael, can't you do that?" Jules asked.

"No, but I know someone who may be able to help. Sans might be the key to all of this. If my mother was funneling money to the medical examiner then maybe my sister wasn't guilty at all. Maybe he died from a heart attack and not the head injury."

"You can go, Michael," Jules said as she walked up to him and kissed his cheek. "Frankie is in very good hands, and you're only a phone call away. Go help your sister."

"I don't want to be the guy who leaves you. I feel like I've already done that, and I never want to do it again."

"I fell in love with you because you're the guy who helps people who need it. Helping your sister is the right thing to do. I'm only sorry I didn't listen earlier to you about the kind of person your mother is. I can't believe I ever defended her."

"You're always looking for the good in people. That's what's special about you." Michael winked.

Betty broke them up with a shooing of her hand and interjection of her wisdom. "And she's just a bitch, that's what's special about your mother. Now go get done what you need to and make sure she can't hurt anyone anymore."

Chapter Thirty-One

"Clara really came through," Michael said as he walked back toward Bobby and Lindsey, who were leaning on the car they'd *borrowed* from Michael's mother. They'd pulled into a field where they wouldn't draw attention to themselves. "Apparently she was as motivated to have a big bust as we were. I don't know what my mother did to her in the past, but it certainly worked in our favor. I've been involved in a lot of cases, but I've never seen people move so fast to issue warrants especially in the middle of the night."

Dr. Sans sat inside the car with wide terrified eyes, looking ready to wet his pants. "The district attorney will be here in a couple minutes to take your statement," Michael explained. "If you cooperate fully and leave out the details of this little incident today, you should get full immunity. You're just lucky the people you're turning in are higher up on the food chain than you. Otherwise you'd never get this deal."

"Okay," he said as his voice trembled. "I'll tell her everything as long as they can protect me from your mother."

"That's not part of the deal. You're getting immunity. You can find your own way to protect yourself from my mother," Michael retorted. "If you tell me everything now, I might be able to help you in that department. The sun's about to come up, and I want to be there when they arrest my mother. I want to know what she did without waiting to hear it in court. I deserve that."

"I would, Mr. Cooper, but without other witnesses here I think you might kill me when you find out." Sans shifted nervously in the car, inching away from Michael.

"Why?" Michael asked, feeling a wave of heat roll over him. "What did you do that would make me want to kill you?"

Just then a car with dark tinted windows pulled up and two agents stepped out, escorting Mary Salinger, the district attorney Michael was expecting.

"I think I'll wait and tell them."

Before Michael could push any further for answers, Mary was at his side introducing herself and beginning the process. "I'd like you to come back to my office, Dr. Sans, and we can take your statement. If the details of your story can be validated, you will be granted full immunity from any wrongdoing. My office is very motivated to address any issues of impropriety and crime, especially when they relate to those who see themselves above the law due to their financial standings. The calls I received on this matter made it clear it was top priority for many people. Apparently Mrs. Cooper has made some enemies over the years."

"I'm sure there's a long list." Michael stepped away from the car and let the agents lead the doctor away. It had been made very clear to him he would have no involvement with this case. He was too close to be in on the details of anything that happened after the district attorney got involved.

"What's the matter?" Lindsey asked, reading Michael's grimace. "This sounds like good news, right?"

"Immunity is a double-edged sword, and every now and then it slices you right open. We might have just let a guy who did something unspeakable off the hook. That's the risk."

"So what do we do now?" Bobby asked, stretching his aching back. They'd pulled an all-nighter trying to keep things contained and contacting all the right people.

"You guys go get us a hotel for tonight. Get a room for Josephine and her fiancé too. When this blows up we'll want to be laying low. I'm going to go back to the house and get Piper and Josephine out of there before the cops come. I'll get our bags and drop them off at whatever hotel you pick. Then I'm going to the hospital to be with Frankie. I can't wait until all this is over and we're on a plane back to Edenville."

"You got it. I'll text you with the name of the hotel. Good luck." Bobby slapped Michael's back.

"I couldn't have done any of this without you two. Thank you for saving my ass. I owe you."

"You don't owe me. You've done so much for me, and my family, this past year. Lindsey, on the other hand, will likely hold this over your head forever. She'll be calling in favors for the next ten years," Bobby joked.

"Actually," Lindsey said, looking up at the sky as if she were fighting a wave of emotion, "this is one of the few times in my career I felt like I was a part of something. I've always wanted to be a cop, but in Edenville, while things are better than they ever have been for me before, it's still a struggle. People there genuinely see me as less than the guy next to me. It was really nice having people other than Bobby trust me."

"As far as I'm concerned you're one of the best on that force. I've seen them all, and they can't hold a candle to you. I'd be happy to pass that along to any of my contacts at the FBI if you ever consider taking your career to the next level." Michael left the offer hang there unanswered while he turned and jogged back toward his car in the big field where they had all parked.

He turned the radio up for the short drive back to his mother's house and let the music pump through him. There was finally some good news to let sink in. His mother would be snarled up in the web she'd been creating most of her life. His sister might just be proven innocent of causing her father's death once the medical examiner was shown to have been bribed. His last text from Jules said Frankie was looking great and ate a good breakfast without getting sick. They were just waiting to hear back from the doctor. The idea of being on a plane back to Edenville was something he could finally envision again.

He pulled up to the front of the house and hopped out of the car. People here weren't used to anyone driving themselves, but Michael had ditched the chauffeur once he knew they'd be up all night. He slammed the car door behind him and tucked the keys in his pocket.

"Don't you want to leave those with me, sir?" the valet asked.

"No, I'm not staying long," Michael retorted as he hopped up the stairs toward the front door. He made his way to the nursery first to pack their things. When he walked in the door he saw Piper and Betty chatting.

"What are you doing here?" he asked, shocked to see Betty away from the hospital.

"Frankie woke up full of fireworks in her eyes and looking for something to keep her attention. That's a good sign, but Jules wanted me to come here and get a few of her favorite little toys since nothing at the hospital was doing the trick. Now I just got a call from her saying they're going to be released. They will be on their way back here in a little while." Betty loaded her bag with a few more chirping and sparkling toys and then started for the door.

"A car just left to pick them up," Piper explained as she helped Betty straighten up the toys.

"It's not a great time for them to come back here. There is a lot going on. Give Bobby a call and see if he can meet up with Jules and head her off before coming here."

"Okay," Piper said, clicking the keys on her phone. "I just sent him a text."

Michael's phone rang with a local number that took a minute to register. "Clara?" he asked as he answered it, and he wondered why she'd be calling. She helped out tremendously with getting the ball rolling with the district attorney's involvement in the case. She'd called in all sorts of favors. But what he didn't expect was to hear from her again. They'd made it clear he'd be cut out of that.

"Where are you, Michael? At the hospital with your daughter?" Clara asked and Michael took note of the fact that she'd paid attention to that part of their conversation last night. He couldn't help but be touched.

"No, I'm at my mother's house gathering up our things."

"Michael, I'm sorry to be calling you but my friend at the DA's office just phoned me. Normally I wouldn't disclose anything as it could compromise the situation, but I feel obligated to tell you this since it could have some medical significance for your daughter."

"What is it?" Michael asked, bracing himself against the wall and drawing Betty and Piper's eyes to him.

"Sans stated on the record that he facilitated in the administration of drugs to make your daughter appear ill in an effort to keep you from leaving. Apparently the medications were put into her bottles and given orally. He also had the nanny put something in her ears to make it look as though her eardrums had burst. I'm having someone on my staff head to the hospital now to brief your daughter's doctor on the types of medications and the doses so they can treat her properly. I'm so sorry to have to tell you this."

"My daughter has been discharged, but please still send someone so the doctor can inform us if there is anything else we need to do." Michael took in a deep breath and tried to keep telling his legs to support his weight. "I can't believe this. This was my mother? She was trying to make Frankie sick so I would stay here and keep her income intact? She poisoned my daughter?"

"I'm afraid so. There is much more to the story that I can't share but know that the doctor is spilling his guts, and your mother will pay. This was the only part I felt I had a responsibility to share with you since there may still be some danger to your daughter's health."

"What about the medical examiner?"

"I can't share anything else, Michael. The police will be there to make arrests soon. I suggest you clear out now. Let them do their job."

"Like hell," he said, more to himself than to Clara as he hung up the phone and launched it across the room with a roar. It smashed into pieces as Betty covered her mouth to silence her yelp.

"She didn't," Piper said, clearly praying what she'd just heard wasn't the truth. "No one is that desperate for money."

"She did. She paid the doctor to poison my daughter and now she's going to answer to me." Michael charged out of the room and down the hallway, calling out for his mother.

"What's going on?" Josephine asked as she stepped out of one of the rooms into the hallway, stopping Michael in his tracks.

"Your mother hurt my child to protect her money. And now she's going to see why that was such a bad idea." Michael balled his hands into fists and tried to move past Josephine.

"How do you know she did that?" she asked, planting her hands on his chest and slowing him down just long enough for Piper and Betty to catch up.

"Because the informant at the DA's office just gave her up." Michael took her wrists and moved her aside.

"Who, who gave her up?" Josephine asked with a quiver in her voice.

"Michael, stop," Piper yelled as she latched on to Michael's bicep and tried to dig her heels in, but instead he just dragged her along.

"Should I assume you've changed your mind and are ready to do what I tell you?" His mother's voice echoed down the long hallway as she stepped out of her own study.

"You can't lay a finger on her. If you do you won't be getting on a plane back to Edenville. We won't be going back to our lives. Please don't do this," Piper begged as Michael inched closer to his mother, seething anger rolling across his face. "How long will you have to go before you can hold Frankie again if you do this? You'd be leaving them both again."

With those words Michael's feet froze. He looked down at Piper's pleading face and realized she was right.

"Are you that southern and uncivilized now that you were resorting to violence?" Tabitha crossed her arms over her chest and looked down her nose at all of them.

"Mother," Josephine started in a frantic voice but was brushed aside by Betty who charged forward angrily.

"Piper is right. We can't lay a finger on her, so how 'bout a fist?" She cocked her arm back and with a loud thwacking noise made contact with Tabitha's nose. The skin on the bridge of her cosmetically sculpted nose split open and began pouring blood. She stumbled backward to the ground and sat there in shock as she looked at the blood staining her pearly white satin shirt. "You best lay right there and not give me a reason to treat you like the greased pig you are."

"Listen you low country ignorant piece of garbage, you will pay for hitting me. I'll make sure of it. To think I was actually nice to you and your ridiculous circus of trash. Your daughter was so desperate to have better than you've ever given her that she'd listen to anything I said. That's what a low IQ will do."

"You think you're a rich woman? You're the poorest person I've ever had the displeasure of meeting. You're not a person at all, you're a pile of DNA that doesn't deserve to breathe the air my daughter does. It is my job to defend my child and make sure no one hurts her, but I am a woman of God who believes that it is not my place to judge or punish a person. However," Betty said, cracking her knuckles and letting her eyes bare down on Tabitha, "the only thing I am more of than a woman of God, is a grandma. I will beat your sorry ass black and blue for what you did to my grandbaby." Betty leaned down and grabbed a handful of Tabitha's hair and the collar of her shirt and began dragging her toward the front door.

"Get off of me," Tabitha shouted, but she couldn't break free of Betty's grip. "How do you know about Frankie?" she asked between yelps of pain.

"Let her go," Josephine yelled as she trailed behind Betty and a bloody Tabitha on their way to the front door. One of Tabitha's expensive shoes came off, followed by an earring that hit the floor with a jingling noise.

"I'm going to hand deliver her to the damn police." Betty dragged her through the large foyer and let her go with a thump against the marble floor. "You better hope they lock you up and throw away the key because the only chance you got is if there are bars between you and me."

Michael looked on with astonishment as the blood continued to trail down his mother's face and Betty seemed ready to pounce again.

"I'm not getting arrested," Tabitha said resolutely as she backed away from Betty but stayed on the floor.

"Yes you are," Piper said, peering out the window as the police cars began pulling in. "They know everything you did, and everyone you paid to do it."

"How could you do this? I'm your mother?" Tabitha asked through gritted teeth as she stared up at Michael.

"You're not my mother. She is," he replied, looking over at Betty and letting the anger slide off his face. Betty had been a mother to him in every sense of the word since the moment he first sat at her table to eat. She'd cared for him. Told him when he was being a fool. Praised his accomplishments. Bragged about him to anyone who would listen. She fed him. She taught him, and she loved him.

At the meeting of their eyes, Betty let her clenched fists relax and her face soften. Michael could tell she'd made her point. She'd done her damage, and she knew it was time for the police to do their job. As droves of people came through the door he watched as Betty stepped back, flattened the wrinkles out of her dress, and then shook the ache out of her hand.

He moved over to her and pulled her in for a tight hug. "You've been everything I've ever needed. Every time."

"I just decked your mother, Michael, don't make me sound like a saint," Betty laughed, but it only made Michael squeeze her tighter.

"You might not be conventional, but you're perfect. I wish everyone in the world had a Betty."

"It would certainly make for lots more good food."

"There would be lots more good everything."

"Mr. Cooper?" one of the officers asked as he pulled a small notebook from his pocket. "We're taking your mother, the nanny, and your sister into custody. I know you are a lawyer. Will you be representing any of them?"

"My sister? Why is Josephine being arrested? I'll certainly do what I can for her. I think as the story unfolds it will become clear my mother was the source of the criminal activity."

"She's been implicated in the conspiracy regarding your father's death. The medical examiner who was paid to falsify his report states that, upon Josephine's request, he added there was a head injury. Your father died of a heart attack. There was no head injury. She'll be facing charges of conspiracy and obstruction to say the least."

"Josephine," Michael gasped as he saw his sister being led from the house in handcuffs. "I don't understand. Why did you say you threw something at him?"

"I needed you to think I was in trouble. You were always a sucker for bailing people out. I figured if you thought I'd go to jail for murder you'd do what mother wanted. But instead you ruined everything." With a fiery resolve she fought against the handcuffs and it took a second officer to pull her from the house.

"She was in on it," Michael said in disbelief. "Why would she do that?"

"Because you become the person who raises you," Betty said, clutching his shoulder. "Unless you are smart enough to get the hell out like you did. Just remember that when you're raising Frankie; she is what you help make her. So make her something good." Betty stepped out the front of the house and Michael stared blankly for moment.

"I can't believe this is what I was born into. How did I end up with these people as my family?" he asked as he followed her outside in a daze in search of fresh air.

"You didn't," Piper replied with a smile as she looked out across the long driveway and saw Betty joining Jules, Frankie, and Bobby who were leaning against a waiting car. "You ended up with those people as your family. And luckily so did I."

"What are they doing here?"

"Bobby was trying to catch Jules before she got here but he couldn't. Once they saw the commotion they weren't going to leave you here. They wanted to be here for you."

Michael put his arm around Piper and amidst all the chaos and police presence walked with his head held high toward the people who'd had his back since the day he'd met them and he was sure they'd be there with him until the end.

The End

Epilogue

Five Years Later

It had become a running joke that Clay and Betty would have the longest engagement in history. Every time they considered getting married something else would come up and, in true selfless fashion, they'd postpone. It had become kind of laughable.

They'd sit on the porch and tell everyone they were happy and didn't need some fancy party to enjoy their lives together. But everyone felt they deserved the party, nonetheless. It had to be something special and unique. Something completely Betty and Clay. Something inclusive of the people and things they loved. Piper glanced around the room and knew they had nailed it.

"It's kind of funny to see what you can accomplish when you're really rich," Piper said, nudging Jules in the ribs.

"We were plenty rich before the money," Jules nudged back. "But yeah, this is pretty nice."

"I'm glad everything is finally out of probate and the money and assets from Michael's family can actually go to good use." Piper took a glass of champagne off the tray as it passed by.

"The majority of the money has been donated. Michael wanted to make sure all the people and charities who should have benefited from it did. But I'm glad there was enough left over for a day like today."

"I've never seen anything like this in my life," Michael laughed as he looked around the room and joined them, Bobby right behind him.

"It's like a hoedown crossed with a sophisticated culinary event. My brain doesn't know what to make of this. Maybe it's the jet lag."

"Well we *are* in one of the most prestigious culinary schools in the world. Clay and Betty are going to get their own private class after the ceremony. Plus, there is no more romantic place in the world than Paris," Jules argued.

"Yes," Michael said, kissing his wife, "I just don't think the L'acadamie de Cuisson would have agreed if they knew how many handkerchiefs and hay bales would be involved in the decorating of their great hall. I doubt they have any idea what half this stuff is."

"Look over at Betty," Piper said as she pointed to the front of the room where Betty, looking beautiful in a simple, white cotton dress, was hugging everyone in sight. "It's perfect."

"It was important that we did it far away from home for that reason right there," Jules reminded them. "Betty wanted Chris, Sydney, and their kids to be with them on such a special day and here they are, getting their hugs. Plus, look at Willow and Josh. They never got a honeymoon either and now they're here in Paris to celebrate. Rumor even has it that Jedda might propose to Crystal under the Eiffel Tower, but you didn't hear that from me." Jules had a look of sheer joy on her face and it made Piper want to hug her. This wedding was quirky and eccentric just like all of the guests in attendance, but Jules was right. It was so perfectly Clay and Betty.

"I think we might be in some trouble with all these kids." Bobby laughed as a gaggle of children chased a runaway balloon across the room. Frankie was the ringleader, constantly reminding the others she was the oldest and the tallest. CJ, Chris's boy, didn't count, Frankie would remind them, because he was pretty much a grown-up now.

But Bobby and Piper's son, Logan, wasn't far behind Frankie in inches, even if he was a year younger. Adopting him and his twin sister, Sky, had been the wildest adventure Bobby and Piper had ever been on and that was saying something, considering what they'd been through over the years. Chris and Sydney's daughter, Hope, was trotting along, chasing the balloon. Somewhere along the way they'd all taken to calling each other cousins, and it seemed to suit them perfectly.

"Do you think they'll be the next generation of troublemakers like we were? Will they chase down right and wrong and think they can save the world?" Piper asked, watching the kids move wildly through the hall.

"I hope not," Bobby decided, pulling his wife in toward him. "I hope their lives are perfectly boring and uneventful. I hope they work at the Wise Owl restaurant for Betty and Clay and keep their noses out of trouble."

Sydney and Chris came up, exchanging hugs and handshakes and clearly excited to share in this day. "Another move planned for you guys I heard," Bobby said, looking somber about that news.

"That's what happens when you're in witness protection, unfortunately," Chris said with a shrug. "But we're thinking of something a little farther away this time. Sydney has only been here for eighteen hours, and she's fallen in love with Paris."

"Please move here," Jules squealed, "because I want to visit!"

"Look, there's Clay," Michael said, pointing to the door in the corner of the room. "It looks like he's ready."

They all gathered in the front of the room as Clay came forward and took Betty's hand in his. There would be no walking down the aisle or observing other traditions. They had said they just wanted to exchange vows in front of those they loved in a place that felt like they belonged.

The minister walked up in front of them and addressed the small group with a prayer, then asked Betty and Clay to profess their love to each other.

"Clay," Betty started, and the small group fell silent, even the children. "You put lard in your biscuits rather than butter, and I still love you. I think that's saying a lot." The small group erupted in laughter. "We are different. Wildly different in many ways. We cook different, we pray different, we clean different, and by different I mean you don't clean and I do." The laughter rose up again. "But we do one thing very much the same. We love the same. It's easy to say the word unconditional, but it's hard to live it. In you I've found someone who loves my quirks and my faults. Today as we come together in marriage, *finally*, I vow to never be dumb enough to screw this up."

"Betty," Clay started, trying to compose himself against the laughter. "Until the day I met you, I'd never met anyone like you. And no one since can compare to you. You've given me so many things over the years. A purpose, a business partnership, love—but there is one thing you've given me that I will spend the rest of my life thinking about."

"Food poisoning?" Betty asked. "Because I'm telling you that wasn't from my grits, you had the *flu*."

"No," Clay shouted, trying unsuccessfully to stifle a laugh. "You've given me all these people." He gestured toward the group. "I'm a grandpa because of you. I've never had the ability to connect with people in any way other than food. My whole life I hid behind aprons and recipes. Then one day a woman burst into my fancy restaurant kitchen, strong-armed me for a recipe, and then stole my heart." He leaned in and kissed her as the group let out an audible teasing groan.

"Oh stop it, y'all. Did everyone do their homework?" Betty asked, pointing her finger at each of them. "I told you all to think of something southern that describes what love really is. I want to hear them. That's your gift to us, and I want some real profound stuff here."

"I'll go first," Chris said, stepping forward and lifting his daughter into his arms. "Love is like wildflowers. It springs up where you'd least expect it and often at times when you didn't know it was coming. But then when it's there you wonder how you ever lived without something so beautiful." Sydney leaned in for a kiss and then blew a kiss over to Betty.

"Love is like a thunderstorm. It's the collision of differences to create something so awe-inspiring you have to stop and watch its power." Sydney smiled.

"Oh my goodness, you fools are going to have a hard time topping that. They really thought it through." Betty laughed with tears in her eyes.

Jedda and Crystal stepped up next. "We worked on ours together. Love is spring. Everything is new and full of life. When you feel like you can't take another day of winter, spring comes to rescue you."

"Can I go on record to say this is weird?" Willow groaned and rolled her eyes. "We didn't make you guys do this stuff at our wedding."

Piper shot out above the voices of the crowd. "You didn't invite any of us. You eloped."

"You're welcome for that." Willow shrugged back. "But fine, I have one. I wasn't in the South very long, but to me love is like a butterfly. It has the capacity to change if you give it time. It needs patience and quiet but then something amazing can be born out of it."

"Born, like a baby?" Betty asked, peeking through the crowd to see Willow's belly to check for any signs of a bump.

"So much for keeping a secret," Josh said, throwing up his hands and laughing. The group paused for a moment to shower Willow and Josh with their celebratory congratulations before Betty called them back to the task at hand.

"That doesn't get you out of having to answer, Josh. Something southern that shows us what love is; get on with it," she urged.

"To me love is like a field. It's wide open, endless space and potential, and you get to choose what you do with it, how you care for it, and what you build on it." Josh placed a hand on Willow's stomach and they leaned their foreheads together as they smiled.

"Michael and Jules?" Betty said, gesturing over to them.

"For me," Michael started, "love is like a mountain. You're forever scaling it and there is no end in sight."

"That's depressing," Jules said with a slap to his shoulder.

"No, because I love mountain climbing. I never want it to end. The important thing is every now and then you look over and make sure your partner is beside you. It's easy to leave them behind sometimes. You've got to go

213

back, help them find their footing, and keep climbing together."

"I guess that's okay then," Jules said as she slid her hand into his. "To me love is like snow in the South. It's special and unexpected, and when it happens you feel like you're looking at something wondrous and magical. It doesn't come along often, but when it does you stop what you're doing to make sure you take it all in."

"That just leaves you two," Betty said, peering over at Bobby and Piper.

"Mine is easy," Bobby began. "Love is a porch swing. It's quiet talks while we listen to the crickets. It's watching the sunset, and occasionally still being there to see it rise. It's comfort and safety and finally having peace."

The whole room waited silently as Piper turned her chin up and tried to think of just the right words. She was the girl who couldn't love and was never loved before. That's why every eye in the room was now trained on her; she was the one who climbed out of the deepest hole to find happiness. Her answer would be more impactful because it would be rooted in her journey from empty to full. "Love is a wagon wheel," she said, biting at her lip to hold back tears. "It's round and infinite if it's done the right way. Its spokes are made up of more than just the two people pledging themselves to each other; they include all the people who help them get there and help them stay there. You are all our spokes, holding us together, keeping us strong, and we hope we do the same for you. I like that our stories don't have one hero all the time. I like that when one of us is down, we've created a village to raise us back up. Eight years ago I accepted an invitation to dinner at Betty's house. That was the day my life truly started, because that was the first day I felt love."

No one spoke for a moment as they all seemed to be taken back by the power of Piper's words. Love had come late to her. Life had been hard on her. But now, looking at her, you'd never know. Every label she'd ever had was now washed away and replaced. Now she went by mommy, auntie, daughter, wife, and friend. Everyone circled around her, and even the kids took part wrapping their arms around her tightly. "Love is a wagon wheel," Betty said, nudging her way closer to Piper, making sure she got a good squeeze in.

Piper closed her eyes and felt the sensation of every arm embracing her. With support like this, she knew she'd never truly fall down again. Love would always hold her up.